JAMES GORDON

Chasing the Sea Hound

This edition first published in paperback by
Michael Terence Publishing in 2023
www.mtp.agency

Copyright © 2023 James Gordon

James Gordon has asserted the right to be identified as
the author of this work in accordance with the
Copyright, Designs and Patents Act 1988

ISBN 9781800945272

No part of this publication may be reproduced, stored
in a retrieval system, or transmitted, in any form or
by any means, electronic, mechanical, photocopying,
recording or otherwise, without the prior
permission of the publisher

Cover images
Copyright © Jickaro
www.123rf.com

Cover design
Copyright © 2023 Michael Terence Publishing

Part One

AD 1683

Chapter I

Carlos Sanchez walked unsteadily down the gangplank from the galleon on which he was the bosun in the service of the king of Spain's navy. He hadn't stepped on terra firma for some weeks and not being used to the ground he was standing on not pitching and rolling made his gait ungainly. It was early summer in the year of 1683, and he was leaving his ship in Cadiz to order supplies for the captain. Although quite early in the day it was already hot and the smell of seaweed, rotting fish and other detritus in the enclosed harbour walls was almost overbearing. He was just making his way to the naval office when he was hailed by two horsemen in uniform. "Would you know of a Naval bosun by the name of Carlos Sanchez?"

"Who may I ask is doing the asking?"

"We are from the his majesty's guard sent by his majesty to accompany him to Madrid at his majesty's request. I have two letters here, one for the captain of his ship which I will deliver now and one for Carlos himself."

"It's your lucky day for I am he." Carlos took the letter, slid his knife under the royal seal and read it's command for him to present himself to the royal residence in Madrid as quickly as possible. "We have a spare horse if you can ride?" said one of the men. "I learned horsemanship as a child although I've not been on a horse for a good many years," replied Carlos.

Ten minutes later he was seated astride a fine looking animal. "Madrid the letter said, that's a fair step, it must be a hundred leagues from here."

"We will be there in less than a week. There are fresh mounts along the road."

"It must be important to come all of this way to fetch me. Have you any idea as to what the king wants?"

"We are not in his confidence. We are told what to do and when and do it no questions, so your guess is as good as ours, my friend." The three of them rode out of the harbour of Cadiz away from the screaming and wheeling gulls, onto the hot and dusty road towards Madrid.

After hours of riding they stopped at an inn. Carlos all but fell from his mount, his legs more used to the rocking of a ship's deck than the rocking of a horse's saddle. One of his companions took care of his horse while the other went inside to see the innkeeper to obtain rooms for the night and the evening meal for the three of them. After a meal Carlos was ready for his bed. He was tired and saddle sore and not looking forward to days of dust, heat and more saddle sores. Morning came all too soon but having had breakfast he felt as if he could endure another day on horseback. His travelling companions had saddled his new mount that had a mind of its own. Not wanting someone on its back it bucked and tried to throw Carlos off. But Carlos was as single-minded as his mount and was determined not to be thrown off, so an uneasy kind of respect was enjoyed between man and horse.

As midday came they rested the horses beneath a small grove of trees and had bread and cheese that one of the king's guards took from a saddlebag and a canteen of warmish water. Carlos was glad to have stopped but did not want to sit down. He was now quite sore and it was easier to walk around under the trees. His horse was in a better mood now after the morning's ride and nuzzled his hand as he held out a piece of bread. An hour later they were all mounted and riding out from the shade of the trees and back on the road for Madrid. Late in the afternoon, in fact nearer the evening, they came to another inn where they stopped for the night. One of the king's guards took care of the horses while the other busied himself with the accommodation and evening meal. Carlos asked the innkeeper if there was a bath on the premises and the innkeeper with a broad grin on his face took Carlos around the back of the inn and pointed out a small river. "Help yourself senor, I'm afraid I can't make it warm for you but it will soothe your saddle sores.

After his evening meal he walked out to the river and

taking off his boots and clothes he dived into the cold but refreshing waters. After half an hour or so he climbed back into his clothes, walked back to the inn and went to bed. The next morning at breakfast the inn keeper asked if he had enjoyed his bath. "Bath," said the guards, "You had a bath," they both said. "Well, we don't do baths but we do have that," he said pointing out of the window to the river at the back. The horses were brought to the front of the inn by a young boy all saddled up and ready for the day's journey. One of the guards gave him a small coin without the guards seeing Carlos give him a bigger one.

They mounted up and headed out into the already hot sun. Carlos was now getting used to the riding and the swim in the river the night before had calmed his saddle sores and his skin was getting hardened to the leather saddle. All of that day they made steady progress up the road to Madrid, but that night there was no inn so they had to sleep on the ground using their saddles for pillows and sharing some more bread and cheese that came from a saddlebag. Sometime in the night the horses started snickering as an unfamiliar scent made them restless in the darkness. The two guards woke Carlos with their pistols in their hands and whispered, "Bandits." Carlos listened to every small noise in the darkness, hearing all sorts of imaginary sounds. Suddenly one of the guards cocked his flintlock pistol and pulled the trigger, the gunpowder flared, then flashed. The peace of the night was shattered by the roar as the musket ball raced on its path into the night, drawing a grunt and running feet in the darkness. The horses settled back down and everyone went back to sleep.

As the grey dawn broke and turned into another hot day, they saddled their horses. Every one of them stiff from sleeping on the ground, they mounted the horses and started the day's riding. They hadn't gone but a few hundred yards when they came across a body lying in the road with what looked like a pistol shot wound to the chest. "Looks like one of our visitors from last night, a pretty good shot considering it was pitch black," said Carlos. "We will have to keep our eyes peeled for his mates. They might come looking for revenge, but I think they were after the horses so they will probably be on foot and won't be a problem. With all three keeping a weather eye open for an ambush by the bandits they continued on along the dusty road to Madrid. Carlos was missing not having breakfast. It was not for the first time in his life and most certainly it wouldn't be the last, but he was having trouble trying to keep his mind from his stomach.

About mid-morning one of the guardsmen rode off, disappearing in the distance to their left. "Miguel has gone to find water and food. There is another inn but we will not reach it until after dark, because we will have to rest the horses for a while in the shade at midday." Carlos noticed dust on the horizon first and Mario checked that his pistol was ready to be fired if need be. As the rider came closer they could see that it was Miguel returning and both men breathed a sigh of relief. The three of them travelled on together, Miguel saying that he had found a smallholding where he had been able to purchase some provisions for them and refill their water bottles. So when they came across some trees that offered some shade with a bit of grass growing beneath they stopped to rest the horses and eat.

After eating fresh bread, ham and hard-boiled eggs with cool water, they leaned against the trees and dozed while the horses nibbled on the grass. Sometime later they mounted their horses and continued on their way and they kept on riding all through the day and into the evening. Carrying on into the night they came to an inn where two roads met. Mario went in and sorted the accommodation and meal while Carlos and Miguel attended to the horses, taking off the saddles and making sure they had water and hay before entering the inn for their meal. After the meal they sat with a tankard of ale. Carlos asked about their life as the king's guardsmen, while Mario and Miguel asked about life on board a galleon and all of the places he had been. When the ale was finished and all of the questions answered, they went to their beds glad they weren't sleeping on the hard ground this night.

The next morning Carlos awoke early to the smell of bacon cooking and the sound of voices. He ventured into the main room surprised to see Mario and Miguel already having breakfast and drinking ale. Carlos joined them at the table and a serving girl brought him breakfast and a tankard of ale. It was dark outside Miguel told him they had made good progress over the last few days and that with an early start they might make it to Madrid that night.

The horses were brought around to the front of the inn where they mounted them and rode off just after the dawn was breaking. They set off at a trot making good time in the cool of the day. For most of the journey so far they hadn't met many other travellers other than the bandits, but now there were people with carts loaded with things to sell at a market somewhere. "Where are all of these people going so early in the morning?" Carlos asked Miguel. "The same place we are going, my friend, Madrid," He answered. All of that morning they rode on, stopping at midday to rest the horses. Miguel bought some fresh bread and ham from one of the travellers as they continued to stream by heading for Madrid. When the horses were rested all three mounted up and trotted up the road. It was dark when they first sighted the lights of Madrid and smelt the smoke. The two guardsmen led the way to the royal residence where they stabled the horses and found sleeping quarters and an evening meal.

In the morning before breakfast, Carlos brushed his clothes, trying to make them look like they hadn't been worn for five days on the back of a horse. When he was finished they looked a little better than when he had started, but there was little else he could do to make them smarter. Giving up he followed his nose to the smell of food. He found both of his travelling companions already eating, so he got some food and sat beside his two new friends. "When do I meet the king?" he asked. "An officer will come and collect you when the king wishes to meet you. It might be in an hour or it could be this afternoon, it depends how urgent his majesty views your meeting to be."

It wasn't long before a guards officer came and found Carlos, escorting him to the meeting after being searched for hidden weapons. When Carlos was presented to the king, the king wasted no time in getting down to business. "Shall we walk in the garden? There are more French and Dutch spies in here than fleas on a dog's back. At least out there we can keep some space between us and them," said the king. "If that is your want your majesty," replied Carlos. When outside and away from other people the king said, "I sent for you because I was informed that you were the best man for the job that I need doing. I need you to sail one of my smaller galleons called the Dinero Espiritu, quite apt for what you will be doing. It is at anchor at Cadiz, ready for you to sail to Veracruz, a port in the Gulf of Mexico."

"I know of Veracruz, your majesty, I was there when I was just a cabin boy," said Carlos.

"Once there you will be contacted by my agents who have some chests that are to be loaded secretly under cover of the night. Once that has been done you will send a messenger to a lady by the name of Rosa Maria Dolores. She is a favourite of this royal court and she will have her friend and maid Isabel with her. You are to wait for her, then set sail to Kingston, Jamaica, in the Caribbean, where she will visit her grandparents, who are my envoys on that island. She will stay for a few days, then return to the ship. You will then return to Cadiz as fast as the weather allows, is that clear, more importantly can you do it?" asked the king. "It will be done as you wish your royal majesty," said Carlos.

"Right, from this moment on you are Captain Carlos Sanchez. I also heard that you were attacked by bandits on the way here, so you will travel back in a carriage with guards. May good fortune travel with you Captain Carlos." With that the king gave Carlos a weighty purse. "That is for your expenses," he said. He then turned and left the garden and returned to his duties.

The officer who had escorted him in appeared and escorted him back out, saying that a carriage and guards will be here in one hour to take you back to Cadiz. Carlos opened the purse that the king had given him. Carlos had never seen that amount of gold coins in all of his life. I shall need a spyglass, navigational instruments and a naval captain's uniform when I get back to Cadiz he thought to himself. Within the hour a coach pulled by four horses stopped beside him. "Captain, your coach. I am informed that you are now a captain, is that right, Carlos?" asked Miguel. "Yes, from a few minutes ago, what are you doing here?"

"I am one of your guards. It is said that there are bandits on the road to Cadiz and we are to get you there safely. It seems that you are now an important person on a mission for his majesty and your safety is now uppermost. Just sit in the coach and take it easy, you won't get saddle sores in there."

Carlos sat looking out of the window of the coach in which they left the royal residence, taking the narrow roads through Madrid passing out into the sweeter smelling country air. They were making better speed with the coach than with Carlos riding a horse. As the day wore on, food and water were passed through the window with them only stopping to change horses. They didn't stop until after the sun had set. When they did eventually stop it was at an inn that they hadn't used on the way to Madrid. Carlos climbed out of the coach, his legs not feeling like they belonged to him. Sitting in a coach all day long doing nothing wasn't as easy as it seemed. Morning came and while Carlos was eating his breakfast the coach was brought around to the front of the inn, waiting for its passenger.

Carlos finished his breakfast and climbed aboard the coach, which set off almost before the door was shut. The day followed the same pattern as the previous day. Food and water was passed through the window without stopping, only pausing to change horses at intervals along the way and finally stopping at an inn after sunset. In the afternoon of the next day the coach pulled into the harbour at Cadiz. Carlos climbed out of the coach, saying goodbye to Miguel and the rest of his escort and sought out the Dinero Espiritu. He found his ship at anchor in the harbour and finding a man with a small rowing boat he paid him to row him out to his ship. Climbing aboard the ship he was confronted by a sentry. "What do you want?" he asked. Explaining that he was the new captain, the man showed him to his cabin. "I want to see all of the crew in the morning. I want to know what stores are on board and how much water, powder and shot.

Carlos made himself comfortable in his new cabin that was to be his home for the foreseeable future. Looking around he found some charts, but not the ones he needed and he made a mental list of the things he would need for the voyage to Mexico. He found an unopened bottle of port and a glass and took a drink before taking a walk out onto the main deck, inspecting the rigging, looking at the masts, spars and poking his nose into every nook and cranny. After a good look around the ship he returned to his cabin, had another glass of port, then lay on the bed and went to sleep. The next morning he walked out onto the deck, finding the crew waiting to meet their new captain. "Right, where is the bosun?"

"There isn't one," said one of the crew "he left with the old captain."

"Okay, find me someone to row me to the shore." When one of the crew, had rowed him to the shore he told him to wait for him and he would be quite a while. First he found a place to eat, as he hadn't had breakfast and no evening meal the day before. When he had finished breakfast he went shopping for the things he would need, a new uniform, navigation instruments, charts and a spyglass. Then he went to the naval office to see about a bosun and any stores that they would need.

Word had reached the office from Madrid that captain Carlos Sanchez was to be helped in any way possible to ensure his forthcoming voyage was a success. "I need a bosun. It seems the bosun from my ship has departed with the former captain," said Carlos Sanchez. "We will find you a worthy bosun in the next two days and he will report to your ship. Anything else you need, it will be our priority, captain."

"Thank you for your help, good day." Carlos carried his new purchases to the crewman and the small boat. "Take me back to the ship," said Carlos. Boarding the ship, Carlos put his purchases in his cabin, went up to the main deck and called all of the crew together. "You will have a new bosun in the next two days. We will get this galleon shipshape before he arrives, then with all stores and water loaded we will leave port for some gunnery practice before we depart for Veracruz in the Gulf of Mexico. Any questions?

After two days of scrubbing decks, mending sails, loading powder, cannonballs, water and other stores all was ready for the journey to the Gulf of Mexico. Carlos called for his small boat and an oarsman to take him to the quayside. Reaching the quay, he told the crewman to wait for his return. First he went and paid for his captain's uniform, then went to the naval office to inquire about his bosun. "He is here ready to start his duties under your command, captain."

"Tell him there is a boat waiting at the quay. I will be there after I have finished my business on shore and he can accompany me on my return to my ship." Captain Carlos went to find some hot food and to buy a bottle of port and when he returned to the boat at the quay the new bosun was waiting for him. "Captain my name is Juan Fernandez bosun assigned to your ship."

"We have been waiting for you, bosun. We will be leaving on the morning tide. Our destination is Veracruz, but first we will be having gunnery practice once out at sea. Now climb in and we will make our way to the Dinero Espiritu." The crewman rowed them back to the galleon at anchor in the harbour.

Chapter II

Morning came clear and bright with a stiff breeze from the east. They weighed anchor and headed for the open sea and making a good eight knots they were soon away from land. Carlos put his new spyglass to his eye and looked in every direction to see there were no ships in sight. "Bosun, make ready the guns both port and starboard." The bosun shouted, "Load," and the crew raced to the guns and readied them for firing. Carlos gave the word and the guns fired. "Now do it again but quicker, bosun." The crew loaded the guns quicker this time. "Fire," shouted Carlos. "Better but not good enough. "Our life might depend on this, so do it again, practice it twice more, bosun." The bosun carried on with the practice, getting quicker each time. "Okay, get back to your normal duties, we have a long way to go."

Carlos went back to his cabin and getting out his new charts he plotted out the course for the 5,600 nautical mile journey to Mexico. If we can average eight knots it will take about a month, he thought to himself. As darkness came Carlos took his sextant up on the deck and established their position. Calling the bosun to find out their speed. The bosun came back with the measured speed. "Eight knots steady captain," he said. Carlos returned to his cabin, marked the chart with their position, direction and speed and sat with a glass of port and wondered what the morning would bring. The Dinero Espiritu was still making good headway in the choppy morning seas. When Carlos walked out on the deck, the crew were hard at work heaving on ropes, adjusting the sails to get the best speed possible. Luckily the wind had stayed in the east throughout the night. "Bosun," shouted Carlos. The bosun came running to greet his new captain. "Morning, Sir."

"Bosun, let's see how quickly you can get the guns loaded, rolled out and fired." The bosun raced off yelling instructions to the crew, who in turn raced to the guns and pushed gunpowder down the barrels followed by a cannon ball. They pushed the cannon out of the gun ports and fired the cannonballs out across the choppy waters of the Atlantic Ocean, splashing into the waves some distance away.

"Okay, bosun, now we are getting somewhere. That was much better. We will keep up the practice in the coming days." Carlos took out his spyglass and surveyed the horizon in every direction, then he checked their direction with the compass and being satisfied he returned to his cabin. He studied his charts, noted the progress they had made and with a satisfied smile he thought that everything was coming together nicely. The lookout in the crow's nest shouted. "Ship on the starboard bow!" Carlos ran to the main deck and taking out his spyglass searched the horizon on the starboard side. There about two leagues away near the horizon he could see the sails of a ship, too far away to make out what flag she was flying.

Carlos kept his spyglass focused a few more minutes on the ship as it came closer, then he relaxed as the Spanish flag came into focus "Friendly," said Carlos. The rest of the day passed without any more sightings or incidents. After dinner Carlos took his sextant and took the readings, checked the compass and asked the bosun for their speed. He returned to his cabin and put the sextant reading onto the chart, when the bosun knocked on the cabin door and came in telling Carlos that the wind had shifted but they were still making seven knots. "Thank you bosun, that will be all." Although the bosun had said they were doing seven knots, with the sextant readings Carlos knew that they were averaging eight knots.

In the morning Carlos noticed that the wind was fitful, blowing steady for a few moments, then veering to another direction, then not blowing at all. Carlos had seen it many times before and knew that this was the calm before the storm. He went to the helm and looked at the compass. They were still heading south-westerly but having to do some tacking. He called the bosun, "Keep an eye on the weather. I am sure we are heading into a storm. Make sure the crew reduce the sail as the wind strengthens. Close the hatches and let me know of any problems." In the afternoon it started raining, but not pouring just light rain that was whipped up by the squally wind that stayed in the east. The sea became choppy but the Dinero Espiritu kept her head up and made good headway, crashing through the waves on her way westward. Carlos left his cabin and walked the decks in the rain making sure that things were in order, sails were set properly and the lamps were lit for the evening. Having checked everything he went and had a word with the helmsman. "How's she going?"

"Fine, captain, riding the water well and on course. Making good speed. The bosun hasn't taken any sail off as yet, so I would say we are making ten or eleven knots."

"Right, keep her steady. Any problems let me know, I'll be in my cabin." Carlos returned to his cabin for his dinner and a glass of port.

As the predawn turned into daylight Carlos took a walk on deck before breakfast and found the weather was much the same as it was the night before. They were crashing through the choppy seas still with full sail and the wind holding with the same direction as it did last night. Leaving the wet and windy weather, Carlos returned to his cabin and breakfast. In the early afternoon the rain and wind abated, leaving the skies a clear blue with a bright sun shining above them. Steam rose from all parts of the galleon under the warm sunshine. Carlos, who had left his cabin and walked out on the main deck and sunned himself, had a smile on his face as he watched his ship drift along, the Atlantic having changed colour from the grey into a deep blue.

Carlos made his way to the helm and checked the compass for their direction. Being happy with what he saw he lifted his spyglass to his eye and searched the seas for any other ships. Not seeing any he shouted for the bosun, who promptly arrived at his side. "Yes, Captain."

"Ah, bosun, the weather is fine and there are no ships near so I think a practice is in order. Let's see how quick the crew can get the guns ready today." The bosun quickly had the crew appearing from the rigging and below decks, loading the guns and running them out and firing out across the empty seas. "Thank you, bosun, that will do. Have the crew return to their normal duties and tell them I am pleased with their efforts." Carlos walked the decks in the warm sun again, well pleased with his life as a captain in his Royal majesty's navy. He spent the rest of the day making sure all was shipshape and Bristol fashion. Seeing all was as it should be he returned to await his dinner and a glass of port.

Dinner arrived and was served at the cabin table and after his evening meal and glass of port Carlos with his sextant walked up on the main deck. With the stars shining in the warm evening skies Carlos took his readings, walked over to the helmsman looked at the compass, seeing they were heading just north of east asked the old crewman to estimate their speed. "I reckon we be doing about four knots, I can get the bosun to tell ye exactly, Captain."

"No, I think you have seen enough years at sea to know how fast we are going helmsman. Thank you and good evening." Carlos returned to his cabin and his charts, marking down their precise position. For two more days they had the nice warm weather. Their speed wasn't record breaking but with only a small breeze they couldn't expect anything else. Then the wind changed direction to blow from the south, which meant they had to do some tacking and the wind speed increased as did the speed of the Dinero Espiritu.

The bosun kept the crew on their toes keeping the galleon on course and as fast as she would go. That day and night they had travelled a good bit further than the previous two days, making Captain Carlos a happy man although he didn't have a set date to be in Veracruz. Every day Carlos took his bearings and marked the new position on the chart. He looked with enjoyment as the distance from their starting point grew longer and the distance to their destination grew shorter taking a good chunk out of the 5,600 nautical miles they needed to travel. But of course the trip would be further than that because wind direction wasn't always favourable for their destination. For the next week nothing out of the usual happened. They kept going westward albeit sometimes south-westerly and others north-westerly. The weather had became warmer as they came nearer to the Caribbean Sea.

Carlos walked the decks in the cooler morning air and lifting his spyglass to his eye he surveyed the ocean from horizon to horizon. He was just on the point of putting away the spyglass when something caught his attention, what looked like white sails on the horizon. It of course could be white clouds above an island, but it was just too far away to be sure. Carlos stayed on deck for the rest of the morning keeping an eye on the white specks in the far distance. In the afternoon they were close enough to see that the white specks were indeed two ships, still too far away to see what flags they were flying.

Carlos called the bosun. "Bosun, load all of the guns but leave the gun ports closed. If those ships look anything but friendly open the gun ports and be ready to fire." The bosun hurried away, calling out instructions to the crew, who in turn hurried to load the cannons. As the two ships came closer neither showed any interest in Carlos's galleon passing by and into the distance behind them. Long after the two ships had disappeared over the horizon Carlos ordered the bosun to fire the cannons to clear them so that no accidents would occur. The crew fired all of the guns, the cannon balls splashing harmlessly into the waves some distance from the ship. As evening came on Carlos took his bearings, took a look at the compass and then went down to his cabin marking their progress on the chart.

One week later they were sailing by small islands in the Caribbean Sea with their white sandy beaches and swaying palms on the edge of bright blue, calm waters. Now he had to sail west keeping north of Cuba and south of America into the Gulf of Mexico then south to Veracruz. With a gentle breeze blowing from the southeast the crew kept them travelling westward. Carlos's day was spent with his spyglass and a sea chart. Keeping watch on the horizon in the warm sunshine wasn't an unpleasant job with a man up in the crow's nest telling him what he could see from his lofty position. They made slow progress with a fitful breeze but at least it was in the right direction. In the evening Carlos took his bearings as he did every evening when the weather permitted, entered them on his chart and calculated how many more days before they saw the harbour at Veracruz.

Morning came bright and warm with a slightly brisker breeze sending the Dinero Espiritu along at a better pace, putting a smile on the captain's face. They left the Caribbean and sailed into the Gulf of Mexico sailing south-westerly. With a fair wind that filled the sails they clipped along at a fair rate, so it wouldn't be too long before they saw the harbour at Veracruz. It took just two more days for the Dinero Espiritu to nose her bow into the harbour. Carlos dropped anchor out in wider harbour, not wanting to tie up against the quay side until he had been contacted by the king's agents. It didn't take long for the news to spread that a Spanish galleon was in the harbour. That night a dinghy with three men made their way across the calm harbour waters. They climbed aboard the galleon in the darkness away from the quayside and found the captain waiting for them. Carlos took them to his cabin and spoke in hushed tones, not wanting to be overheard by any of his crew, most of whom he knew were cut-throats and vagabonds not to be trusted, although he needed some of them to help load the secret cargo.

The three men left the galleon unseen by anyone, climbed into their dinghy and rowed away across the dark water. The next morning Carlos called the bosun. "Yes, Captain, what are your orders?"

"Make a list of the provisions that we need and

gunpowder, shot and such like, then later this afternoon I want you to tie us up against the quay wall."

"Yes, captain, it will be done." That afternoon the galleon weighed anchor and with little sail crossed the harbour to the quay side and tied up. Carlos went on shore and ordered the provisions that they needed to be delivered the next day. The sun was hot and the usual stench from the harbour wasn't pleasant. It seemed no matter what port you were in, in whatever part of the world, that smell was the same. It invaded your nostrils and even seemed to enter the body through the pores in the skin. That night one of the men from the dinghy boarded the galleon again, and made his way unseen to the captain's cabin. "Captain Carlos, all is in place for the cargo to be loaded, have your men ready to bring it onboard at midnight tomorrow night."

The next morning the provisions started to arrive on the quay side and the crew toiled in the hot sun stowing it all below deck. Carlos then sent a message to the lady Rosa Maria Dolores, who lived some distance away, that her ship was docked in Veracruz harbour. The messenger said that he knew the lady and would leave immediately to deliver the message. Spurring his horse away, he kicked up a small dust cloud as he left on his mission. Carlos hated waiting but wait he had to, so he paced the decks of his ship. He had now been waiting for five days, since arriving from the Spanish port of Cadiz. His passenger was the royal court favourite Rosa Maria Dolores, returning to Spain via the West Indies. Carlos was not happy about carrying a woman on his ship, as it had long since been considered unlucky. He had little say in the matter as it had been a royal command. All of the trip provisions had been loaded, along with the secret cargo that his crew had loaded in the dead of night away from prying eyes, not that his crew were to be trusted made up of cut-throats, thieves and those fleeing from the law.

Carlos wanted to get out to sea to the relatively clean air, away from the stink of rotting fish and other detritus that littered the harbour streets. The lady Rosa was taking her time getting to Veracruz. Carlos had sent a messenger to her residence some two-hour horse ride away from the port when he had arrived. The days for the crew were spent repairing sails and scrubbing the decks. Captain Carlos kept the crew sober by throwing those who got drunk into the filthy water of the harbour then keeping them in the sun for a few hours with no water. Four days later a mule train arrived with Rosa Maria's effects and a message that she would arrive at the port in a few days. The crew loaded the lady's luggage on board, while Carlos had a rant at anyone unfortunate enough to get anywhere near him. But he could do nothing. After all, he was here by the command of the king to bring this lady home to Spain.

It was six days later in the afternoon when Rosa Maria Dolores rode into the town along with her maid and more luggage. "Good afternoon my lady, Captain Carlos Sanchez at your service," he said with a bow of the head. "You have a cabin for myself and my maid?"

"I am sorry my lady but this is a warship. You will have my cabin but I'm afraid you will have to share it with your maid. I feel sure you will find it adequate my lady. Anything you need I will do my best to accommodate you. Have a nice trip."

"Bosun, make ready, we leave on the tide," came the captain's voice. Later as the afternoon faded into the evening and the tide reached its high mark, the bosun shouted "Sails." Sailors sprang up the rigging and, walking across the spars, undid the canvas sails, securing them to a lower spar. The hawser were unfastened from the quay and Dinero Espiritu slowly, very slowly turned her bow towards the harbour and open water on the ebbing tide.

The sails hung limp as the temperature dropped and the sea breeze changed from onshore to offshore. The sails began to flap and the pennants flutter and the warship headed out into the Gulf of Mexico on her way to the West Indies and then Spain. Lamps were lit while the crew still swung about in the rigging adjusting ropes and sails. Sometime after midnight a light north-westerly breeze sprang up bringing a smile to captain Carlos's face, softening his up-till-then grim features. He spoke a few words to the bosun, then retired to a hammock, having given his cabin and comfortable bed to the lady Rosa and her maid. An hour or so after dawn the lady Rosa walked the deck of the ship, not being able to sleep because of the rolling of the ship and the creaking and groaning of the constant movement of wood and ropes. She stared out into the seemingly never-ending expanse of blue water all around them, all land left behind in their wake.

Captain Carlos walked those same planks of the deck, trying to ease the aches and pains from sleeping in the hammock. He engaged the lady Rosa in polite conversation as he passed her on his morning stroll along the deck of his ship. The lady Rosa returned to the captain's cabin to see if the maid had found something for their breakfast. The maid had packed in one of the trunks in the last of their luggage some things that she had thought that they might need on the voyage.

Undoing one of the trunks she unpacked bottles of red wine, cheese, ham, fruit, pickles and biscuits, followed by silver plates and goblets. Rosa entered the cabin to see all the things that her maid had packed. "You are a treasure, Isabel, if it hadn't been for you I'm sure I would have been eating ship's biscuits and drinking grog along with the crew." After having breakfast the two women took a walk along the deck of the Dinero Espiritu, which was not making great headway with the light north-westerly breeze. Rosa thought it would take until Christmas to reach the Indies if the wind didn't start blowing stronger than this. Captain Carlos having walked his aches and pains off encountered the two ladies watching the horizon for land, but all they could see was the sun sparkling off the small waves on the flat calm waters. "Hello, captain, I trust all is going well." He flashed a smile that didn't reach his eyes and said "We are making progress, given the weather conditions. I'm sure we shall have some stronger wind presently."

Captain Carlos walked on, giving orders to those unfortunate enough not to see or hear him coming. Others had disappeared up the rigging pretending to make adjustments to ropes and sails. Carlos wasn't the happiest of men when the wind chose not to fill the sails. He liked a bit of a blow, as he would say to the bosun. In the afternoon it looked like the captain was going to get his wish, as clouds appeared on the horizon behind them and the temperature dropped by several degrees. As the afternoon passed into early evening the wind began to strengthen followed by a rain storm. The ship turned into a different animal. It was like a greyhound, the sails billowing, it seemed to enjoy the driving rain. It surged through the building waves, pushing a bow wave in front of it. All through the night and the next day the wind howled through the rigging and rain lashed the decks, so the ladies nor the captain walked the decks of the now sprinting galleon Dinero Espiritu.

At the end of the second day the storm blew itself out and the sun set on the horizon in a spectacular blaze of red, orange and yellow, promising a beautiful day for tomorrow. There was a gentle breeze that night and the warship made good speed of about six knots eastwards through the hours of darkness, towards the West Indies. The morning brought calm seas, bright blue skies and a warm southern breeze. Although the wind was from the wrong direction, with the skill of Captain Carlos Sanchez, the bosun and the crew, they kept the three decked, three masts floating gun platform pointing in the right direction. The ladies, having had their breakfast, took to walking the main deck, as was becoming the norm on clement days. The two ladies thought a little exercise might be a good thing whilst being cooped up on this long voyage, although they would be able to be more active on the stop in the West Indies.

The days passed slowly as they crossed the Gulf of Mexico and out into the Caribbean. Now they had to change direction to the south going down the western coast of Cuba to Jamaica, then around the south coast to Kingston. These waters were dangerous waters, with ships from enemy countries and pirate ships flying the skull and cross bones. There was a crewman with a spyglass in the crow's nest from dawn to dusk, keeping a weather eye on the seas all around the Dinero Espiritu as she fought against the southerly wind. A call came out from the crow's nest, "Ship on the port beam three leagues." The crewman kept the captain informed of the progress of the sighted ship, while other crewmen were getting the guns ready for action at a moment's notice.

The weather was hot and the breeze stayed in the south sometimes swinging to the south-west. Rosa Maria and her maid walked up and down the main deck aware of the tension in the air, knowing that another ship was heading in their general direction. The hours seemed to pass more slowly but as the evening closed the tension eased as darkness was seen to be a friend. The captain took a reading with his sextant and the compass, plotting his position and course, hoping that by the morning the other ship had either gone or was close enough to identify. All that night the crew had to tack to keep the ship heading southwards against the breeze. As the grey light of dawn lightened the sky in the east the wind shifted into a more easterly direction making it a little easier to sail southwards and gaining a little more speed. As the day brightened there was no sign of the other ship and the tension in the crew's faces and the way they went about their duties seemed to have relaxed. Even the captain seemed to be of a better disposition with even a smile for the ladies as they passed him on their walk around the main deck.

It took another four days before the crewman in the crow's nest shouted that he had the coast of Jamaica in sight. Captain Carlos ordered a direction change to port taking them eastwards towards Kingston. The crew worked like a well-oiled machine, climbing the rigging and hauling on ropes with the bosun spinning the ship's wheel. The Dinero Espiritu changed her course, at the same time gaining a little more speed and the crew kept a weather eye open for any ships carrying the skull and crossbones flag of pirates. This part of the Caribbean was a hot spot for them looking for easy targets, not that Dinero Espiritu was in any way an easy target with her thirty cannon and well-trained crew.

As they passed along the south coast of the island, Rosa and Isabel could see its white sandy beaches dotted with swaying green coconut palms. As the afternoon passed into evening, the captain decided to anchor in a big sandy bay, so all sails were lowered, lamps lit and the anchor set. The galleon rocked gently in the small swell and light breeze in the large sandy bay and everyone was looking forward to the next morning when they would drop anchor in the harbour of Kingston town. The crew were looking forward to the delights of the town, the captain had business of his own, not naval or the royal household, just perks of being the captain. The lady Rosa had people to see and things to do, so would take her maid with her. The dawn brought forth a beautiful bright sunny day. Captain Carlos scanned the sea from horizon to horizon, shouted for the bosun to weigh anchor and the warship sailed through the sparkling blue waters into Kingston Harbour.

Captain Carlos dropped anchor in the middle of the harbour, thinking it safer here, than tied up to the quay, for he didn't want prying eyes watching what he was doing, not that what he was going to do was illegal since he was just getting rum and cigars. The carriage stopped at a large house with verandas all around the building on two levels. Rosa and Isabel alighted from the coach and instructed the driver to return when they sent word by messenger in a few days. The two women walked up the path and knocked loudly upon the heavy wooden door, which was opened by a maid who enquired as to who they were. "Tell the lady of the house that Rosa Maria Dolores wishes to see her."

"She doesn't take unannounced visitors, if you would like to make an appointment."

"Tell the lady of the house that her granddaughter is here to see her. I think she would probably like you to show us in."

The maid quickly showed the two ladies into the library and then disappeared to the rear of the house. The lady of the house walked into the library, took one look at Rosa and a broad smile spread across her face.

"Rosa, my Rosa how did you get here?"

"It's a long story, grandma, but where is granddad?"

"He is in the garden. It is the best place to be, as there is a refreshing breeze that blows down from the hills. Who is this, Rosa?"

"I'm sorry, grandma, this is my friend and maid Isabel. She is my travelling companion on route from Mexico to Spain. We are travelling aboard the Dinero Espiritu now anchored in the harbour, one of the king's naval warships, commanded by the Captain Carlos Sanchez. We are here for a few days."

"Come into the garden. I will get Clara to bring refreshments."

All three of them walked through the house into the garden to where Rosa's granddad sat in the morning sunshine. "Who was the caller?" he asked as he turned around. "Rosa, is that really you, where on earth have you sprung from? Come let me look at you."

"They, that is Rosa and Isabel, are on one of the king's naval ships going home to Spain from Mexico and are here for a few days," said Rosa's grandma. They all sat in the garden telling stories of their lives since they had last been together in Spain and Rosa told her grandparents about life in the royal court and her trip to Mexico, where she had made a considerable fortune, most of which had already been sent back to Spain and how the king had arranged for Captain Carlos to bring her back to Spain via the West Indies to visit her grandparents.

Rosa and Isabel spent the days relaxing and enjoying good food and wine, enjoying the company of Rosa's grandparents. On the day they were leaving, Rosa's grandfather gave her a small package, telling her to open it when she was back on the ship and to keep the things inside close to her. The coach arrived as arranged and they travelled back to the harbour. A small boat took the two ladies back to the warship where captain Carlos was waiting for them.

Chapter III

As the tide was high Captain Carlos spent little time in getting the bosun to make ready to leave. The ladies watched the crew climb up the rigging, walk across the yardarms, set the sails, haul on ropes and get the ship underway. They left the harbour and turned eastwards following the southern coast of the island, with its white sandy beaches, gently swaying palm trees and warm blue waters. A brisk south-westerly breeze filled the sails blowing the Dinero Espiritu in an easterly direction before clearing the island and turning north-easterly towards Spain and home. Rosa and Isabel left the main deck and returned to the captain's cabin, undoing the parcel her grandfather had given her. Inside was a beautiful emerald pendant in a gold setting with a small inscription on the back, Rosa Maria Dolores, a fine granddaughter AD 1683. The other item was more sinister, a small knife in a sheath designed to be worn on the inside of a woman's wrist. Isabel undid the buttons on Rosa's dress sleeve and fastened the sheath to her left wrist with the two narrow leather straps, doing up the buttons again until there was no sign of the knife.

From that moment on Rosa wore both of the gifts in her every waking moment. She loved the emerald pendant and the knife made her feel a little safer on this ship full of men. She had seen the looks she and Isabel got as they walked the decks of the ship, looks that didn't leave much to the imagination. But what could they do? There was no way they could stay cooped up in the captain's cabin for the long trip back to Spain. For two days they made their way into the Atlantic Ocean, leaving the warmer waters of the Caribbean Sea. Early on the third day the lookout in the crow's nest sighted a ship some two leagues away on the starboard side. Captain Carlos with his eyeglass studied the ship, trying to make out the flag she was flying. The lookout shouted down that he thought it was either French or Dutch. As the hours passed it became clear that it was a French flag she was flying and she was not as large as this Spanish warship so Captain Carlos dismissed it as no threat to them.

The French ship was captained by a man named Jacques Devereaux, a licenced corsair by the French King. They caused havoc in and around the West Indies ports, but were not considered a threat to the big gunships. But Jacques was not just any old corsair. He had studied gunnery and had had two long-barrelled cannons made and fitted to his ship so that they could fire directly to the front. The smaller ship shadowed the Dinero Espiritu always staying behind on the starboard side. Captain Carlos ordered the bosun to make ready four cannon on the port and starboard sides. The crew speedily had the guns ready like a well-oiled machine. The bosun said, "Do you think they are a threat, captain?"

"They would be insane to attack us. They can only have ten guns and they would be slaughtered in a broadside," answered the captain. Jacques Devereaux was no idiot, he was never going to get his ship The Sea Hound, or as he called it the Chien de Mer, in a broadside gunfight with this thirty-cannon Spanish warship.

Jacques Devereaux smiled to himself as he looked at the two forward-facing long guns sitting at the bow of his fighting machine, the Chien de Mer. He knew his ship was faster, could turn quicker and outmanoeuvre this Spanish warship. He just had to wear it down. "Load the port long gun," he shouted to his crew. The long guns were awkward to load but worth their weight in gold on this smaller ship. "FIRE!" he bellowed. The gun erupted in smoke and flames as it fired its cannonball across the waves hitting the Spanish ship by one of its gun ports on the starboard side. Captain Carlos was dumbstruck to say the least. He couldn't believe that the small French ship would open fire on a warship of this size. But the thing that worried him more was this ship could fire forwards and that he had no answer to. Jacques Devereaux ordered the crew to load the starboard long gun. The Spanish ship veered to the port side just as Jacques thought it would. "FIRE!" he shouted again. Again there was an eruption of fire, smoke and noise and the cannonball struck the Spanish ship, ripping a hole in the woodwork and causing unknown damage on board.

Evening came on and Captain Carlos hoped that they could get away from the French ship during the night, because he was worried that he would have no answer to the forward-firing guns. Jacques' only worry was that he would lose the Spanish ship in the darkness, but he was going to do something about that. Jacques called his carpenter up on the bow. "Can you make one of the long guns fire in a slight upward trajectory?" he asked "Yes," said the carpenter. "Can you have it done before the dawn?"

"I will need lamps and some help but yes I can do it."

"Take as many crew as you need but not the gunners. I will need them tomorrow morning bright eyed and bushy tailed." The carpenter started work collecting the men, tools and wood he would need. Jacques had made sure they had loaded wood on board ship before they had left France. Being a belt and bracers kind of guy, he had tried to think of every outcome. After all, this was a dangerous occupation.

The carpenter had worked most of the night but was pleased with the result of his and the men's toil. In the grey light of dawn Captain Carlos's worst nightmares were realised, for there no more than a mile away sat the Frenchman. Carlos called the bosun. "Make ready all guns and see if you can get any more speed out of this ship." The bosun gave his orders and the crew raced away to do as he ordered. Jacques leisurely had his breakfast, then called his gunners and instructed them to bring up some chain shot and place it by the modified long gun. The French ship closed the gap between the two ships effortlessly, staying out of range of their guns. "Load the modified gun with chain shot." Manoeuvring his more nimble ship into the position he wanted, he ordered it to fire. The cannonballs chained together had the desired affect, ripping through rigging sails and spars, causing chaos aboard the Dinero Espiritu.

"Reload!" shouted Jacques. Waiting for the smoke to clear he moved his ship a little to the port. "Fire!" Smoke and flames again erupted from the gun and when the smoke had cleared Jacques looked at his handiwork. Pandemonium had broken out across the water on the Spanish ship, with the crew cutting ropes and clearing broken spars and cutting away sails that were hanging into the sea, slowing the ship like it was dragging an anchor. Two of his crew, using the chaos, stole away aft to the captain's cabin. The first of them tried the cabin door and found it locked. Taking his sword, he forced open the door and taking out his gun walked into the cabin. Leaving his mate as lookout, he crossed the room to where the two ladies stood. He didn't take any notice of Rosa's hands as she unbuttoned the cuff of her dress. "What do you think you are doing breaking into the captain's cabin. He will have you flogged."

"Don't worry about the captain. He has his hands full at the moment." He walked up to Rosa, taking her face in his hand. That was the last thing he would ever do in his life except fall to the floor. For like a cobra striking the knife her grandfather had given her had left its hiding place at her wrist and with two lightning-fast strikes had ended his life.

Isabel picked up his gun that he had dropped and the man who had been the lookout looked in the open door and saw his mate lying dead on the cabin floor. He took out his sword and stepped into the cabin. "You," he said. "You will both die for this." Isabel pulled the trigger of the gun she was holding and the sailor his eyes wide as the pistol ball hit him in the chest, fell to the floor dead beside his mate. Rosa cleaned the knife and replaced it at her wrist. Outside, Captain Carlos had managed to clear the decks of the debris. With the loss of some of the sails the ship had slowed and Carlos knew that it was just a matter of time before the French boat opened fire again. He knew that although his ship was bigger and better armed he was a sitting duck, unable to fire a shot at his aggressor, who it seemed could fire at will and he knew would.

Captain Carlos was just waiting for the conclusion to this sea battle when Jacques made a mistake. He had let the Spaniard's ship steal the wind from his sails. Carlos manoeuvred his ship into a broadside position and the Frenchman with no wind in his sails was at the mercy of the bigger ship, who now opened up with all of the cannon that could be brought to bear on the now helpless Frenchman. Jacques was not beaten yet, because the Spanish ship was so much bigger most of the shots were flying too high. The Frenchman opened up with his port side cannon putting shot after shot into her hull, but having to take some hits of his own. At that moment the wind shifted a little, allowing the French ship to fill her sails and move out of harm's way. The Sea Hound had lost the top of her mainsail and her hull was holed but none below the waterline. The carpenter would earn his pay again this day, said Jacques to himself.

Carlos knew that the Frenchman would never make that same mistake again and he didn't have enough sail to get away from him. He cursed under his breath that the Spanish had not learned from history. In 1588 they had sent their armada to England with big ships, but the English with their fire ships and smaller boats had scattered the superior force. The Spanish still built big ships and here he was, Captain Carlos Sanchez of the Spanish navy, being taught a lesson by a smaller French ship. Perhaps fortune would smile on him and they would somehow escape, but he wouldn't put money on it. He walked the deck, looking out across the vast expanse of the Atlantic Ocean at a small French ship with holes in it that he couldn't defeat. While the carpenter was making running repairs to the ship Jacques took out his log and wrote down the events of the day as he had done since leaving port in France. Time had marched on and the afternoon sun dipped towards the horizon. The two captains each had their dreams, Carlos that he would escape in the darkness, Jacques that he had inflicted enough damage that the galleon couldn't escape. Tomorrow, both men thought, was another day.

Dawn brought a dull, cold, stormy day with bigger

waves with white caps. Carlos put his spyglass to his eye and it didn't take long to find the French ship no more than a mile away heading in his direction. It wasn't as fast as it was yesterday, but then again nor was his. Carlos hadn't seen Rosa or Isabel for quite a while. They hadn't walked the decks while the French ship was firing at them, not that he had expected them to. He decided to go to his cabin and check on them to make sure they were alright. After all, they were the King's passengers. When he reached his cabin he saw the damage to the door and then the two bodies on the floor. He didn't need an explanation. He knew these two men, knew how they treated women. "I'll get someone to clear this mess up, are either of you hurt?"

"No," replied Rosa, "we are not harmed." Captain Carlos went out of the cabin onto the deck. Finding the bosun, he told him to get some of the crew and bring up the scum that lay on my cabin floor. "Give them a decent sea burial." The bosun gathered four crew members together and told them what to do. They went to the captain's cabin and knocked on the broken door. "We have come to remove the bodies," said one of them. They entered the cabin, picked up their demised crew mates and left, going up onto the deck. Once on deck they cut the bodies' purse strings took out their gold earrings and threw the bodies overboard into the deep grey Atlantic Ocean.

Jacques came up behind the Dinero Espiritu and had the non-modified long gun loaded. He got his ship in position and fired the gun, peering through the smoke he saw his cannonball dive into the sea as his ship slid down a wave. "Load the gun again," he said. The crew quickly loaded the gun, "Fire!" shouted Jacques. This time as the Chien de Mer climbed up another wave his shot went harmlessly over the galleon. "We will have to wait for this weather to blow itself out and the sea to calm down before we try again," he said to his gun crew. The bad weather lasted for another two days and the two ships done what repairs they could while they journeyed north-eastward.

The next day was calm and sunny with hardly a cloud in the sky. Even the ocean had turned to a blue instead of its normal grey. Captain Carlos put his spyglass to his eye, only taking a few minutes to find the French ship a couple of miles to the east. He prepared his crew for what he knew was going to happen, then he went down to his cabin and told the ladies not to go walking on the deck, for it would soon turn into a battlefield. Jacques steered his ship towards the Spanish galleon, steadily gaining on it in the light breeze, coming up on it from the stern. "Load the long guns," said Jacques. When the guns were loaded he put his ship in the best possible position and he told the gunners to open fire. The two cannonballs found their target, as did the next two and the two after that. Jacques surveyed the damage after the smoke had cleared. Two holes had appeared close to one of the gun ports and another sail hung from one of the masts.

Jacques altered his position, sailing down the other side of the Spaniard. With the guns loaded again he commenced firing at the helpless ship. Salvo after salvo he fired until he could no longer see the Spanish ship for the smoke from his two long guns. Jacques called a halt to the firing, waiting for the smoke to dissipate in the gentle breeze. The Spanish ship had suffered severely from the onslaught, the modified gun doing its part as more sails were hanging useless and the crew were cutting them down and throwing them overboard. The spars and yardarms were splintered and shattered, the masts looking like pine trees after a hurricane. The wind was never again going to push this ship anywhere. Jacques decided to chance another broadside, but first he was going to fire a few shots so that the smoke would cover his intentions. He knew that the galleon wasn't going anywhere anytime soon.

The Chien de Mer opened fire again. As the smoke thickened Jacques altered his position he sailed down the starboard side of the Dinero Espiritu firing all of his port-side guns, reloaded, firing, reloading and firing again. Before the Spaniard could fire a shot the Frenchman had passed by and out of danger. When Jacques could see through the smoke again he saw that the galleon had lost two more of her guns having taken direct hits and the hull with more holes. He could see dead and injured men being put on the deck ready for a quick burial at sea. All of that day the Frenchman fired into the galleon, causing chaos and broken bodies until as the evening approached the firing stopped to let the dead find their final resting place.

The next morning the two ships were no further than two hundred yards apart. The galleon looked strange in the early morning light with its rigging torn to pieces and its sails missing. Jacques summonsed the carpenter and when he came on deck Jacques asked him to put the modified gun back into its original position as there were no sails to fire at. While the carpenter set about his work Jacques gathered the crew together. "Today we finish this fight. Get your grappling hooks, muskets and swords ready. We will fire the long guns, then we will close in, drop the sails use the grappling hooks and board the galleon. I want ten men with muskets on our deck to fire at any Spaniards who choose to show themselves and I want the captain taken alive for ransom is that understood?"

The carpenter finished the long gun and the gunners loaded both guns while Jacques sailed into position. "Here they come," were the only words Captain Carlos had time to say before the guns started firing. For twenty minutes the guns took their deadly toll on the galleon and its crew. Then the Chien de Mer sailed alongside the galleon and grappling hooks were thrown, pulling the two ships together. Men climbed the ropes and boarded the galleon while Frenchmen with muskets shot any Spaniard who was brave enough to show himself. The sound of sword against sword and the sound of pistols firing came from every part of the Spanish ship and the crew with the muskets and Jacques then boarded the galleon. Within an hour the sounds of the battle had ceased and Jacques started lowering the chests that had been loaded on the galleon in the night at Veracruz and the rum and cigars from Kingston.

The two ladies who had been unharmed during the days of battle were gently lowered along with Captain Carlos onto the deck of the Chien de Mer. Jacques went below deck of the galleon to the powder room and there he set a slow fuse using a candle and some gunpowder. He reappeared a few minutes later and cut the ropes securing the two ships together. The sails were hoisted and the Frenchman sailed away to the north-east. After about half an hour there was a large explosion onboard the Spanish ship and the Silver Spirit sunk to add to the growing collection of ships on the floor of the cold grey Atlantic Ocean.

Chapter IV

Jacques showed the ladies and Captain Carlos to a cabin next to his. "You are free to walk the deck and no one will threaten or interfere with you or they will have a long swim back home." It was a sunny afternoon with a westerly wind and the Chien de Mer pushed through the water at about three knots per hour. Jacques sat at his desk in his cabin writing in his log all the events of the day, then went out on deck, took some measurements and compass directions and returned to his cabin to enter them in the log. His attention then turned to the wooden chests that had been taken from the Dinero Espiritu. The first chest as he expected was locked. He went in search of one of his crewmen who at one time had been a blacksmith. "Pierre, I have a job for you, come with me." Pierre followed Jacques to his cabin. "Pierre, I want you to open every one of these chests that we took from the Spaniard, can you do that for me?"

"Yes, but I will need some tools," he answered. "Do you have these tools on board?"

"Yes, I will go and fetch them, Captain," he replied. A few minutes later he returned with a hammer, chisel and what looked like two bent pieces of wire. He bent over the first chest and inserted the two pieces of metal into the lock, moving them about, giving one a twist until the lock popped open. He then turned his attention to the second of the pair of locks on the chest, performing the same action on the second lock and in a minute had that lock undone.

"Where did you learn to do that, Pierre?" asked Jacques. "Let's just say I wasn't always a blacksmith," replied Pierre. Jacques walked over to his desk, picked up a glass, half filled it with Jamaican rum and handed it to Pierre, who gulped it down greedily. "Open the rest of the chests and I'll give you another drink." Pierre set about his task and within an hour had all of the chests open. Jacques fetched the glass this time full of rum. "Here, Pierre," he said handing over the rum, then undoing his purse and tossing Pierre a small gold coin. "Do you smoke, Pierre?" asked Jacques. "When I have the chance," replied Pierre. "Here have this," said Jacques handing Pierre a cigar. "Thanks, Captain, I'll be getting back to my duties then. Picking up his tools he made his way back to the deck.

Jacques opened the first of the chests and had to take a step back because the sight before him was awesome. The chest was filled with gold doubloons or pieces of eight as the pirates of the area called them and some silver coins. As he stood looking at the chest there was a knock on his door. He quickly closed the lid, walked over to the door and opened it to see Rosa standing there. Rosa, looking into his cabin, said "Ah Captain I see you have my chest."

"It is no longer your chest Rosa, but mine," said Jacques. "Well, I hope my dresses will look good on you, Captain. I can't wait to see you in them."

"Which of these chests is yours, Rosa?" Rosa pointed out one of the chests. "I will take a look. If it contains what you say it does I will get two of the crew to bring it to your cabin. Now what did you want me for?"

"Oh, I was just going to let you know that Isabel and I intend to take a walk out on the deck. We need some exercise. Will that be okay?"

"You don't need to ask my permission. Just be careful."

Rosa turned and walked back to her cabin and collected Isabel they took a walk out onto the deck. There was a light breeze and warm sunshine and after an hour or so they returned to their cabin to find Rosa's chest in the middle of the cabin. "How did you get one of your chests?"

"I asked the captain for it. I told him I would look forward to seeing him in one of my dresses, as that was all there was in it. He said he would have a look inside and if it contained my dresses he would have the crew bring it in here."

"I will unpack it for you Rosa," said Isabel. "No, leave it Isabel, there is a little more than my dresses in there."

"No, I packed that chest myself. I know what is in there."

"I had that chest made for me, Isabel. It has a false bottom very cleverly concealed. It contains some jewels and gold that I put in there before you started packing it." Isabel."

"Are you sure that it is still in there, Rosa? Let's make sure." Isabel took out all of the dresses and when the chest was empty Rosa pressed a button concealed just under the inside lip of the chest. The false bottom lifted a little. Rosa pulled it upwards and there was the hidden treasure still in place. "Right, Isabel put the dresses back in there and I will lock it. I still have the key."

In the meantime Jacques was opening all of the chests. They all contained similar items and together they were worth a king's ransom. Jacques thought to himself, I'm rich, even after giving the king of France half. Jacques went in search of Captain Carlos and found him on the fore-deck looking at the two forward facing long guns that had spelt disaster for his ship. They had a bore of not much larger than a man's fist but packed a massif punch. Carlos thought that perhaps at close range they could fire a cannonball right through a ship from port to starboard. "Could I have a word with you, Captain, in my cabin," he asked. "What is on your mind, Jacques?"

"If we go to my cabin there will be a drink of something warming and a nice cigar, with no one listening to what we say."

"Okay, Captain, but I have little to say to you. After all, you are little better than a pirate."

"In your eyes that may be true, but I bettered you with a smaller ship, less guns and a smaller crew. I have no hatred for you captain, you were just an adversary, nothing more nothing less, so do we have that drink or not?"

Captain Carlos gave it a minute's thought then agreed to Jacques' request. They walked back to Jacques' cabin, where glasses of rum were poured and cigars lit. "What is on your mind, Captain Jacques?"

"I have opened all of the chests that you see in here, so I know what they contain. My question to you is why? Why would a Spanish galleon, a warship, be carrying a king's ransom in gold and silver?"

"I was summonsed by the king to take charge of the galleon Dinero Espiritu which you probably know means silver spirit. His majesty thought that very apt. I was to board the ship at the port of Cadiz and sail to the port of Veracruz in the Gulf of Mexico. There I was to collect some secret chests, load them aboard unobserved and then send a messenger to the court's favourite, the lady Rosa and her maid and await her arrival. Then I was to return her to Spain via the port of Kingston, Jamaica.

The lady Rosa's grandparents live on that island and this was an opportunity not to be missed so I procured the fine things we are enjoying now for myself as a perk of the job you might say. We sailed from Kingston where you came upon us. The rest as they say is history.

So now you know the whole story."

"So, the lady Rosa is more valuable than it would seem. I will have to take great care of her and make sure nothing or anyone would do her harm."

"I would think that would be a very sensible course of action, Captain." said Carlos. After Captain Carlos had left Jacques' cabin Jacques took out his ship's log and wrote the story down in great detail along with present speed, course and weather conditions, then locked it in his desk. Jacques went in search of Pierre again and found him making repairs to a piece of ironwork and said, "Pierre, come with me." They walked to the stern. "I have need of you again. No it's not to unlock things that are locked. The two ladies that are on board, I want you to keep a close eye on them. They are more valuable than I at first thought. Make sure that none of the crew goes near them. Tell me if any do and I will deal with them. I will reward you each day, is that understood, Pierre?" Pierre agreed and returned to the piece of ironwork he had been beating with a hammer.

The days passed by with the Chien de Mer making steady progress across the Atlantic Ocean. One morning about a week after the last day of the sea battle, the sails hung slack, not a breath of wind was there, they were at the mercy of the current, drifting slowly along. They came across a fog bank unlike anything Jacques had ever seen before. They drifted into it and it enveloped them like a giant white sheet, making it impossible to see from one side of the ship to the other. All of that day they drifted with only the splashing of the water against the hull breaking the eerie silence. Captain Carlos met Jacques at the wheel. Jacques asked Carlos, "Have you ever come across anything like this?"

"Well, of coarse I've seen my share of fog banks in different places, but this is different somehow. It's not cold or warm. It's so thick you can almost eat it and the sea is like a mill pond. No I haven't seen anything quite like this."

The next morning when Jacques went out on deck the fog was still there, even thicker if that were ever possible. No readings could be done because the sky was somewhere above the fog bank. Two of the crew had climbed to the top of the tallest mast but still could not see anything. The compass was the only thing that gave them any idea of where they were going. Jacques had to admit that he had little idea as to where they were. The crew were getting restless with no work to do and a restless crew was a dangerous crew. Jacques started wearing two pistols and his sword. The day passed slowly with not a glimmer of daylight, just this blanket of fog.

On the third day of the fog, Pierre went to see the captain. "Captain, there are a couple of the crew that are taking an interest in the ladies, hanging around their cabin and whispering to each other."

"Okay, Pierre, thanks. I was expecting it, I will take care of it. Help yourself to a glass of rum." When Pierre had left the cabin Jacques locked his cabin and was about to knock on the ladies' door when he noticed that the door was ajar. He pushed the door open to find one of his crew holding Isabel and Rosa holding a knife to the throat of another crewman. Rosa with her dark eyes blazing was telling the man holding Isabel to let her go or she would spoil his friend's day. "Let him go," said Jacques to Rosa. Rosa let the crewman go and put her knife back in the sheath strapped to her left wrist.

Jacques led the seamen out of the cabin, pointing his pistols at their heads. "You were a lucky man. That Rosa would have made you wish you had never opened her door. What were you doing in her cabin?"

"She invited us in."

"Of course she did. I suppose you were just passing the cabin and thought you and him would just pass a couple of hours swapping yarns."

"That's right, captain, that's exactly what happened."

"Right, well let's take a walk in this murky weather and let me think about what I should get you to do to make amends."

"Anything, captain, anything," said the two men. The fog lasted for another two days. The first thing that changed was a shout from one of the crew at the top of the mast that he could see the sky. A couple of hours later the fog was behind them but there were some ominous black clouds on the horizon. One good thing was the wind had picked up, filling the sails and pushing the ship eastwards at a steady pace. Jacques took his bearings, compass directions and speed. Soon he knew where they were. The storm came upon them with wild winds and lashing rain. The sails had to be lowered or they would have been torn to shreds. It became as black as night. All hatches were closed and the only man on deck was the helmsman.

Chapter V

Pierre came to see the captain reporting that two of the crewmen were missing. "Have you searched the whole ship for them?"

"Yes, Captain, they are not on board, I'm afraid they have been washed overboard."

"Thank you, Pierre, I will put it in the log but we can't send out anyone to search or we will end up losing more men. You can hardly stand upright out on the deck." Jacques had no intention of searching the ship, for he knew exactly where the two missing crewmen were and they wouldn't be coming back. Nobody disobeyed Jacques Devereaux and lived to tell the tale.

The waves were forty feet high and keeping the ship facing into them was a constant struggle. The helmsman could not afford to let her get beam on to the waves, for that would be a certain sinking. Jacques braved the weather to go and see the helmsman and with the rain and spray he was soaked before he had taken more than a dozen unsteady steps. The helmsman was freezing and almost dead on his feet when Jacques reached him. "I'll go and fetch some help. Hang on for two minutes." The captain turned and went to the crew's quarters. "I want two big men on the helm now!! You can change every two hours and keep her head into the wind or none of us will live to see another day."

The two men and the captain made their way to the wheel, relieving the half-dead helmsman, the two big crewmen on one side of the wheel apiece. Jacques and the freezing helmsman made their way to the captain's cabin. "Right, let's get you something to warm you up." He gave the violently shivering man a glass of rum, put a blanket around his shoulders and sat him in a chair. "Sit there and warm yourself. If you want a smoke there is a cigar on my desk, a gift from Captain Carlos," he said with a smile. After an hour the helmsman had warmed enough to go back to his quarters, "Thanks, Captain. I'll be on my way now."

The one thing Jacques hated was not knowing exactly where he and his ship were. When they were in the massive fog bank he didn't know where they were. Now with this storm he was lost again, not only lost but heading into more dangerous waters. Being lost in the mid-Atlantic was one thing with nothing to hit, no land for thousands of miles in each direction. But they were no longer in the mid-Atlantic now. There were other ships and rocky shores to run into. It rained relentlessly, the wind howled all of the day and without sails the wind still blew them along at a steady pace. The waves were mountainous but the helmsman kept the ship's stern facing into the wind. Jacques went out onto the deck as the night drew on, getting soaked to the skin in just a few minutes. Everything looked to be in order, so not being able to help in any way he returned to his cabin, checking that the ladies were alright on the way. The night passed noisily with the wind whistling through the rigging and ropes slapping against the masts. Thunder rolled all around and sometimes right overhead, lightning flashed between the heavy clouds splitting the inky blackness and lighting the deck of the ship. The Chien de Mer kept moving north-easterly closer and closer to danger, as the Atlantic narrowed into the English Channel. Jacques' educated guess said that they were now in the channel. There was no way of knowing for sure. Jacques wrote in his log that they were lost for the present time as the storm clouds covered the sky from morning to night.

In the morning gloom the whole crew were watching the port side as a new sound found their ears, the sound of breakers smashing into rocks. One of the crew shouted from the bow, "Rocks dead ahead." Jacques shouted to the helmsman to steer hard to starboard, but the ship was now too close to a huge overhanging rock formation with what looked like a large cave beneath. Jacques ran down to the ladies and Captain Carlos. "Get on deck now." He raced into his cabin and wrapped his log in waterproof sail cloth and fastened it to his belt and filled his purse with gold coins from one of the chests to go with the small French gold coins already in there. Racing back on deck he was just in time to see his ship strike the rocks around the overhang and the black hole of the cave entrance. The waves were relentlessly crashing against the rocks as Jacques crossed the deck to the starboard side and jumped into the cold water. The last thing he saw was his ship being pushed into the cave by the breakers. At the same time a massive landslide above the overhang brought the overhang crashing down, covering the cave entrance.

The storm passed. One day later an old soldier injured during the wars was doing his usual beach-combing and came across the body of a man on the beach. Looking at his clothes he guessed him to be French, having seen lots of them during the war. He took his sword and purse and was just walking away when he saw something tied to his belt, which he untied and took with him. When he reached the hovel that was his home he sat outside in the weak sunshine looking at his prizes. First he looked at the sword. It had been in the sea water and needed to be cleaned and oiled. The scabbard would need some work but being an ex-soldier it was something he had once been used to. His travelled eye told him that the sword had been made in Paris by a well-respected swordsmith. Next he undid the Frenchman's purse, which it was heavy with a few French gold coin's and a many Spanish Doubloons.

The old soldier had never seen so much money in one place at one time. He went inside his hovel and he took out the smallest French coin from the purse. Then with his knife he dug a hole in the earthen floor and buried the purse, stamping the earth flat again. He returned to his seat outside and unwrapped the package that had been tied to the Frenchman's belt. It was a book of some sort and it was of no use to him as he had never learned to read and write. He rewrapped it, took it inside his hovel and placed it under the straw mattress on the rickety old bed that he slept on to keep it dry. The next day he took the book and the gold coin to the church to see the preacher, giving the wrapped-up book to the preacher and asking him what it was.

The preacher took the wrapping off of the book and studied if for some moments. "What is it, sir?" asked the old soldier. "I don't quite know, it is written in I think French, where did you get it?"

"I came across a dead man on the beach. He had tied it to his belt, I brought it to you. He needs burying sir."

"I'll get someone to attend to the body."

"One other thing if you don't mind. Opening his hand he held out the small French gold coin. Please could you get this changed into our coinage. If I try I shall get cheated. No one will cheat a preacher, will they?"

"Where did you get this coin?" asked the preacher. "It was wrapped up with the book," he lied. "Perhaps I should keep it to pay for his burial," said the preacher. "He has a gold earring to pay for that, preacher if you hurry," replied the old soldier.

Jacques Devereaux's body was loaded onto a cart and taken to the undertaker, where the preacher took his gold earring. The next day the preacher walked down to the old soldier's hovel, where he found him outside warming himself by a driftwood fire. He sat himself down and warmed himself he said, "I have done as you asked," handing the old soldier a small leather purse. "It is a fair exchange for the gold coin you gave me less a couple of pence for my trouble. As for the book it will be kept in the church for safety."

"Thank you preacher, has the Frenchy been buried yet?"

"He will be interred this afternoon if you care to come to the church."

"I am not a religious man but perhaps I owe him, so I will see him laid to rest, preacher." That afternoon Jacques Devereaux's body was laid to rest in an unmarked grave in a small churchyard in the county of Cornwall England. Abe Trevanion watched as the coffin of the Frenchy was lowered into the grave up against the church wall and beside a spreading yew tree.

Abe for a long time had walked the beach every morning picking up whatever the sea threw upon the sand. His injured leg had seen the end of his life as a soldier. Now that he had money he would make sure this grave would not be unmarked for long. He would put the Frenchy's purse to good use. Abe first bought a fishing boat and hired two men to do the fishing. Then he bought the point, the cove and an area of land beside them. Then one year later, he had a mason erect a headstone on the unmarked grave. Life was good for Abe Trevanion from that point on.

Part Two

Chapter I

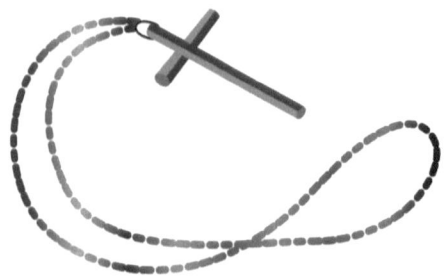

The Franks twins, Samantha and Benny, lived with their parents Tony and Joan, in a semi-detached house close to the city centre of Norwich, Norfolk. Samantha, blue eyed and fair haired and was considered to be the clever one, went to an all girls school a short bus ride from their home. Benny on the other hand was impish and red haired and went to the local middle school, at the age of thirteen, they both enjoyed their particular schools. Tony Franks worked as a train driver on the northeastern line, while Joan worked as an estate agent for a local estate agency. For most of the time everything worked like clockwork, with either Tony or Joan were at home when Samantha and Benny were not at school.

The problem came during the long school summer holidays, when neither parent could take the six or so weeks away from their respective employment. At a family meeting it had been agreed that if it were possible that they would go and stay with their uncle and aunt, Tom and Dora Trevanion, who lived in a small fishing village on the Cornish south coast and could never have children of their own. So it was hoped that the twins could spend the summer holidays down in Cornwall. Tom had his own small fishing boat, catching mostly crab and lobster, while Dora sold his catches and fish from other boats. Dora was also famous for her home made sandwiches and Cornish pasties that she sold from a rented shop.

Joan Franks phoned her sister Dora after the family meeting, asking if Tom and herself could have Samantha and Benny for the school summer holiday period. Dora, with excitement in her voice, agreed spontaneously. Joan asked,"Don't you need to ask Tom first?"

"No, no, Tom, would love the chance to have the twins down here for awhile. It's not that often that we get a chance to see them. Will you and Tony get a chance to come down at all?"

"We might be able to manage a few days towards the end of the summer holidays. Depends on work. You know how it is trying to get time off from the rat race. I have to work all hours and it's much the same for Tony, but I'll let you know if we can manage a few days. It seems an age since we last came down."

"Right, I will get the bedrooms freshened up. Are you going to bring them down in the car, Joan?"

"No, Tony will get the train tickets and give them taxi money. It will be a bit of an adventure for them, and they are clever enough to find their way around the underground in London and catch the train from Paddington."

"I will pick them up from the station down here in the van. Just give me the travel details," said Dora. "Thanks, Dora, you always were my favourite sister."

"You only have one Joan, the same as me!!"

"That's got that sorted then, Tony! Dora and Tom will be only too pleased to have the twins, and Dora will pick them up from the station down there. Will you sort the train tickets for me please, Tony?"

"I'm not in until ten tomorrow. I'll get them before I start work. Have you told the kids yet?"

"Give me chance, I've only just got off of the phone. I'll tell them at breakfast tomorrow and I've got to give Dora the travel details when you have the tickets."

At breakfast the next morning Joan told the twins that Uncle Tom and Aunt Dora were more than happy to have you down in Cornwall for the summer holidays. "So I want you on your best behaviour and please remember your manners. It's not all kids that get the chance to be down at the seaside for six or so weeks."

"Okay, mum we will be on our best behaviour. We won't let you down. It will be fun if the weather is nice."

"You will enjoy yourselves no matter what the weather is like, I would put money on it. Your aunt isn't going to let you get bored. There are thousands of things to do even though it is a small place.

Two weeks later the twins were woken early by their dad. "Come on you two it's time for breakfast. I'm glad we done the packing last night, otherwise you would never have caught the train. Now hurry up, you have things to do, places to go and people to see and that train won't wait for you."

"Okay, Dad, we are on top of it," said Samantha in her usual unfazed manner. "Dad, don't get your knickers in a twist, or you'll give yourself a heart attack. Remember your blood pressure."

"There is nothing wrong with my blood pressure, young lady. I have to have regular medical check-ups with my job." Smiling at their father they sat down at the kitchen table thinking how easy it was to wind up their dad. "You had better have a good breakfast. It is going to be a long day, so better to get started with more than a slice of toast and a cup of tea. Samantha had cereal while Benny opted for bacon, egg and fried bread.

With breakfast done it was time to walk to the railway station, so with backpacks on and pull-along cases they set off, leaving their comfort zone behind. When they reached the station their dad gave each of them an envelope. "Here, put these away in your pockets. It's your tickets and some money for your holidays and we have sent Tom and Dora money for you, as we thought it safer than you carrying a lot with you. Well have a good time, don't get sun burnt and stay out of trouble. You might want to go back some time. Love you. Me and mum will try to get down for a couple of days. One last thing, Brendon, a friend of mine, will see you onto the train."

The twins pulled their cases into the station leaving

their dad outside, a railway man walked up to them. "You must be Samantha and Benny!" he said, smiling. "I'm Brendon, a friend of your dad's. I said I would look out for you. Your train leaves from platform three at 08:04. You have your tickets?" The twins nodded. "Right this way, let me help you with those cases." Getting their tickets out of the envelopes their dad had given them, they followed Brendon to platform three. "That's your train. You timed that just right, no hanging about waiting for it to come. You will be on your way in two minutes. Have a good trip," said Brendon, opening the door and putting their cases in.

The train left the platform at exactly 08:04 and then Benny took the envelope out of his pocket to see what else was in it. There was money and a note from mum, with instructions about what underground trains they would need to get from Liverpool Street station to Paddington station. The note also said that there was a packed lunch and drink in their backpacks, as the train had no buffet car and it would save them having to buy anything. "Sam have you got a note from mum as well?" asked Benny. Samantha gave him that look she gave whenever someone shortened her name to Sam. "I don't know, I haven't looked have I?" The train picked up speed as it left the city and headed into the countryside. Benny loved the wide-open space outside of the windows. Samantha was a city girl, loving the bright neon signs and the lit shop windows. The hustle and bustle of busy shopping centres was her life's blood. Benny wondered how she would cope with a little fishing village in Cornwall for six or so weeks, thinking she is going to be bored senseless.

As was expected the train pulled into Liverpool Street station just short of two hours after leaving Norwich, they pulled their cases along the crowded platform towards the exit. Seeing a sign pointing to the underground they followed in the footsteps of scores of hurrying people heading in the same direction. Samantha and Benny followed the signs to the tube station, using their tickets to get through the gates. Studying the underground maps they soon found their way to the right platform and boarded the train going in the right direction. They had to change tube lines to get to Paddington, but it didn't pose any great problems and they arrived at their destination unscathed.

On Paddington main line station the train was at the platform, but would not leave for another ten minutes to continue their journey to Cornwall. They put their cases and backpacks on the train and found two seats by the window. Samantha said, "I'm going to get something to eat and drink from that cafe over there, do you want anything Benny?"

"No thanks," replied Benny. Samantha said, "Why not? You are always hungry?"

"Well, if you had bothered to read the note from mum in the envelope that dad gave you this morning, you would know mum made you lunch and put it in your backpack along with a drink, so no I don't want anything, thanks. "Okay, Benny, give me a break will you! I'm sorry I didn't read the note. I'll do it now."

"It's no big deal. Mum just thought it would save you the bother of getting something on the way."

Two minutes later the train lurched, then slowly left the station for its five and a half hour trip to Penzance. Benny undid his backpack and took out his lunch and drink as the train made its way out of the city and into the countryside, bringing a wide smile to his face. Benny unwrapped his sandwiches. His mum had done him proud. They were what he would have done for himself. Two each of Marmite and peanut butter and two of plain crisp plus an apple and a bottle of orange. "I don't know how you can eat rubbish like that," said Samantha. "Easily, said Benny. I just open my mouth, put it in and start chewing. You should give it a try sometime."

"Never, I'd rather starve than eat that stuff."

"You probably will. Let me guess, it's rabbit food with cottage cheese and a yogurt right? I've seen more meat on a butcher's pencil than on you."

After eating his lunch the clitty-clack of the wheels on the lines made Benny sleepy, so he leaned back in his seat, closed his eyes and drifted off to sleep. Samantha on the other hand had thoughtfully packed a book, so after eating her own lunch opened her book and drifted off into the world of the writer. A while later Samantha lost her grip on the book and it slipped into her lap. Her head bent forward so that her chin rested upon her chest and she rocked from side to side with the swaying of the train. Benny awoke, stretched and looked out of the window at the countryside. Then a broad grin spread across his face as he noticed Little Miss Perfect, fast asleep, swaying from side to side with her book in her lap. She is going to have a painful neck when she wakes up, thought Benny.

True to Benny's prediction, when Samantha awoke some 20 minutes later she could hardly move her neck. "What's the matter, Samantha?" asked Benny. "A pain in the neck," said Samantha. "Nothing new there then," replied Benny with an impish grin."

"It isn't funny. It hurts," said Samantha trying to rotate her neck. Benny advised, "Careful doing that. Your head might fall off and roll off under one of the seats."

They both settled back watching the scenery pass by the window, now and then catching glimpses of the sea. The train slowed as they came into Plymouth station then stopped for a few minutes. Benny got out and stretched his legs on the platform, then let Samantha do the same. Samantha climbed back onboard and closed the door just as the guard waved the train away from the station. As the train gathered speed and headed out into the countryside, the view was more and more of the rocky coast and sparkling sea. Although they lived not too far away from the sea, this was much different. In Norfolk there were flat beaches of sand or shingle for miles. Here, what he could see from a moving train was wild rocky stretches of coastline, with white-crested waves crashing against them while in between were small sandy coves. He had read in the last few days before the holiday about Cornwall's history. He learned about the wild moors, the tin mining, the shipwrecking and the smuggling.

He was going to enjoy this holiday, but he wasn't

quite so sure about his prim and proper sister. As the train made its way westward they passed old engine houses with their crumbling chimneys, the remnants of long-ago tin mining communities. The train slowed as it came to its and their journey's end. It slowly pulled into the station, and as they passed slowly along the platform, there was Aunt Dora waving as she spotted Samantha and Benny at their window seat. The train stopped and Aunt Dora opened the door from the outside, giving them both a long hug, then helping them with their luggage and they walked out of the station to Dora's van. "Sorry about the fishy smell, but this is what I use for work. You will get used to it after a while." They loaded up the cases and the backpacks and set off for the trip to Aunt Dora's house along narrow little roads with steep banks on either side of the road, having to dive into passing places, because the roads were too narrow for two vehicles to pass each other without them.

After about half an hour of hair-raising driving they came to a small fishing village. "Here we are then," said Aunt Dora pulling into the drive of what looked like a small old fisherman's cottage. They unloaded the luggage and stepped into a surprisingly large building. "This used to be two houses but we bought them both and knocked them into one so there is plenty of room. You have a bedroom each with a shared bathroom. Will that be alright?"

"Yes auntie," they replied. When Benny saw the size of his bedroom he was shell-shocked, for it was at least twice the size of his at home. This will be alright he said to himself. He unpacked his clothes and put them away, then went downstairs to the large kitchen. There sitting at the kitchen table was Benny's Uncle Tom, having his dinner as he went to bed early to catch the early morning tide. "Hello, Benny, my have you grown since the last time we met. If you don't mind an early start tomorrow, you can come on the boat with me and Ivan and try your hand at fishing."

"That would be great," said Benny.

Chapter II

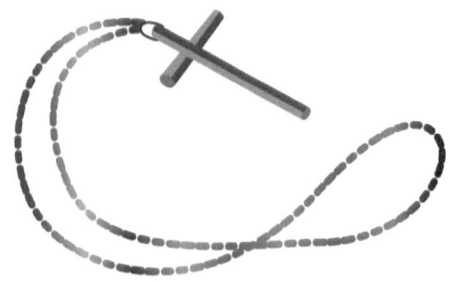

Early the next morning Benny was awakened by his uncle saying. "Up and at them, time and tide wait for no man. We leave on the tide in an hour. Bring a coat. Although it's summer it sometimes gets a cold wind out there. There is time to wash and have breakfast if you are quick." Benny was out of bed in a flash, showered and had breakfast without keeping his uncle waiting. Tom and Benny set off on the short walk to the harbour on a bright sunny morning that promised to be warm. Tom pointed out his fishing boat, a blue and white medium sized craft that looked well cared for but at the same time well used.

As they neared the boat a young man was loading lobster pots onboard. "Morning, Tom, looks like it might be a warm one today."

"Morning Ivan, this here is Benny, my nephew. He will be joining us today. Can you find him a life jacket?" Tom and Benny boarded the boat and Ivan came out of the cabin and gave Benny the life jacket. "Here you are, Benny. Put this on. Can you manage, or do you need a hand?"

"No I can manage. I have used them before. I live not too far from the sea in Norfolk and have spent quite a bit of time on the broads."

"Ah, a sailor in the making," said Ivan. With three of them working, all of the pots and other equipment was soon loaded and Tom and Ivan took the little boat out of the harbour, increasing speed and heading for the deeper water.

"Have you done any sea fishing, Benny?" asked his uncle.

"No Uncle Tom," answered Benny. "Right, firstly drop the uncle. I'm Tom, him over there is Ivan and you are Benny, got that?"

"Yes Uncle… I mean Tom."

"Okay, we need some bait, so if you will grab that fishing rod," pointing to a short fishing rod by the side of the cabin, "I will give you your first lesson. Two things to know about the fish you will be catching are, firstly they are greedy and secondly they are daft. If you look at the line you will see that there are some silver hooks on there. The mackerel the fish you are going to catch think that is something to eat so they almost catch themselves. Right, Benny, just drop the line in the water and let it sink, then just lift the rod up and down keeping your finger on the line and when you feel a small tug reel it in." Benny did as instructed and having felt a tug lifted the rod and reeled in the line. Much to his surprise he had two fish. "Hey, we have a fisherman here, Ivan," said Tom. "Right, Benny put them in that bucket and catch some more."

"How many do you want?"

"Keep going until I tell you to stop," replied Tom.

Benny kept on catching the fish while Ivan baited the lobster and crab pots and Tom was piloting the boat to the pots that they had dropped off yesterday. The morning was getting warmer as the sun sparkled off of the flat calm sea, the only things disturbing the peace and quiet being the thump, thump, thump of the diesel engine and the sound of the bow wave as it passed along the boat's hull. The boat slowed and Tom shouted to Ivan to get ready for the first of the pots. Benny watched as Ivan retrieved the first of the pots, which had a lobster in it, but it was too small so had to be returned to the sea. "How do you know if they are large enough or too small?" asked Benny. "I can do it by sight now but there is a gauge in the cabin in case they are borderline, and there is another gauge for crabs. Females with eggs are also put back," replied Ivan.

Tom let Benny have a go at taking the crabs and lobsters out of the pots and using the gauge to measure them, if they were to be kept then securing their claws. When all of the pots had been checked Tom took the boat to another location where the freshly baited pots were to be dropped over the side. Tom then took them to a place he liked to fish and when they reached it Tom stopped the boat and let it drift. Ivan made coffee in the little cabin and Tom produced sandwiches from his coat pocket that Dora had made before Benny had got out of bed that morning. Ivan baited the hooks on three fishing rods and they all sat fishing and having their lunch. Benny had just got his sandwich to his mouth when he felt a jolt on his fishing rod and the reel started screaming as the line was stripped off of the spool. "Give him a hand, Ivan, he's got something sizable on there and keep a hold of him. We don't want to be fishing him out of the water."

Ivan put his arms around Benny's waist and gave him instructions, as Benny pulled the rod up hard and reeled in the slack line. "That's it boy, keep pumping that rod like that," said Ivan keeping a firm grip of him. Benny was beginning to tire and his arms were aching, but he was making some headway as the fish, whatever it was, was tiring faster than Benny now. A few minutes later the fish broke the surface of the water, threshing about from side to side. "Keep its head out of the water if you can, Benny and pull it into the side of the boat." Benny pulled with all of his remaining strength and as the fish touched the side of the boat Tom grabbed it by the tail and wrestled it into the boat. "What is it?" asked Benny. "That, my boy, is a tope! "What do we do with it?" asked an excited Benny. "Measure it, weigh it, take some photos of it, then put it back in the water."

After all of the excitement, Ivan baited the hook again and Benny dropped it over the side. "Do you think I can have my lunch in peace before you do that again?" said Ivan. Benny had forgotten about his sandwich and coffee, which had now got cold. "Want a fresh cup?" asked Tom. "Yes, please," said Benny. They spent another hour or so fishing, catching some other fish more suitable for sale in Dora's shop. Then Tom started the engine and asked Benny into the cabin.

Right, Benny your turn at the wheel. "You mean I'm going to drive, Tom?"

"I think they call it piloting, but yes take us back to the harbour. Just head for the coast over there," he said pointing to a point on the horizon. Benny took the boat back to the harbour entrance, then Tom took over and moored it against the quay. They unloaded the fish and Tom phoned Dora, who appeared a few minutes later with Samantha in the van.

"Hello, Samantha, have you had a good day with Dora? This is Ivan my crewman. You can come out in the boat tomorrow if you fancied it. Benny caught a sizeable tope today," Tom said, showing Samantha and Dora the photos. "Hey, that's bigger than you, Benny," said Dora. "It weighed more than him as well," added Ivan. They loaded the fish into Dora's van. "You had a good day by the looks of it," said Dora looking at the lobsters, crabs and the line-caught fish. Tom, Ivan and Benny then spent another hour cleaning the boat ready for the next day's fishing. Tom and Benny walked back along the harbour, Tom talking to some of the other boat owners and telling them about Benny's tope and showing them pictures on his phone. "Big un," said one of the men. "Well, as you can see it was bigger than him," said Tom. "You can come along with me tomorrow, might bring me a bit of luck," said the fisherman. "Bad day then?" asked Tom "I've had better. I'll bring the catch over to Dora in a while. "If you want to take up my offer anytime boy, you come and see me. The names Eddie and that's my boat next to Tom's." Tom and Benny walked on home in the glorious afternoon sunshine.

Tom went into his workshop behind the house and started work on a model ship. Benny watched from the doorway. The model was of a square-sailed three-masted galleon. "That is a lovely thing, it looks just like the pictures I've seen of the ships from the Spanish Armada that we did in our history lessons and the ships in "Pirates of the Caribbean."

"This is the third one that I've worked on."

"What do you do with them?" asked Benny.

"I sold the last two. I put them in Dora's shop, people see them and make an offer for them and Dora sells them."

"How long does it take you to build one, Tom?"

"That depends on the weather and the time of year. Sometimes it's too rough to go fishing, so I spend more time in here."

"How do you know how to build them?"

"I've got a set of plans in here somewhere," said Tom. "I saw them online and sent away for them. They give you step-by-step instructions, I buy the wood and sail cloth and the rest I make out of things I find."

Benny was enjoying watching Tom working on his model boat when Dora and Samantha arrived home from the shop. "Hey, Samantha, come and take a look at this ship that Tom is making."

"Don't you mean Uncle Tom Benny," said Samantha. Benny replied, "Tom told me to drop the uncle."

"That goes for you as well Samantha," said Tom, looking at her from his model. "Aunt Dora said Dinner will be ready in 45 minutes," said Samantha. "Tell her that we will be there dreckly," replied Tom. "Dreckly, Tom, what does that mean?" said Samantha a little confused. "Well, I suppose it should mean directly, but down here it means sort of sometime." Samantha went back to the house to tell Aunt Dora what Tom had said. "I'll give him dreckly when he comes in here," said Dora with a smile. After dinner Aunt Dora said, "phone you mum." Samantha phoned home and told her mum about her day and said goodbye giving the phone to Benny, who told her all about his gigantic fish and helping on the boat. He told her he was going out on the boat again tomorrow and Samantha was going too, then he said goodbye and said he would phone again in a couple of days.

Chapter III

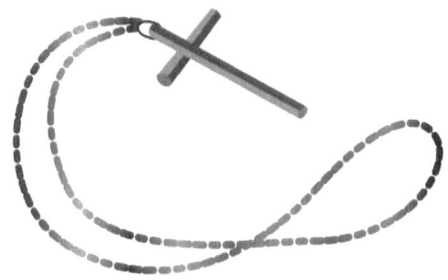

The next morning Tom woke Benny for another day on the boat. Dora said that Samantha would like to spend the day with Tom and Benny on the boat after breakfast and the making of sandwiches,Tom, Benny and Samantha walked down to the harbour. The sky was blue with no clouds, not as warm as yesterday but with the promise of a fine day. When they got to the boat Eddie was on his boat. "Want to come with me today, boy?" he shouted to Benny. Benny replied, "Not today Eddie, thanks, but I'll keep it in mind."

"Who is he?" asked Samantha. "Oh, just a fisherman friend of Tom's who thinks I would bring him some luck if I went out on his boat with him."

"Hello, who's this then, Tom?" asked Ivan taking a breather from his work.

"This here is Benny's sister, Samantha and she is coming out with us today, Ivan. I hope that will be alright with you. I know your feeling about women on boats, not that I'm of the same mind." Ivan pulled a bit of a face but agreed to let Samantha spend the day onboard. Ivan said "I'm Ivan. Nice to meet you Sam." Samantha looked all around and said "Who's Sam? I don't see anyone called Sam. My name is Samantha, not Sam, Ivan."

"If you think that I am going to call you Samantha, all day think again. If you don't like Sam I will call you Manth. Benny was very surprised that Samantha didn't raise any objection. In fact she had a slight smile on her face. "I could grow an old man having to keep calling you Samantha," said Ivan. "When you two have quite finished, perhaps we could get on with the day's work," remarked Tom.

They cast off the mooring ropes and Ivan gave the boat a push on the bow before jumping onboard. They set off out of the harbour, then increased their speed once out of the speed limit. The sea was like a millpond again. Benny showed his sister, now called Manth, how to fish for mackerel, telling her what Tom had told him the day before. It wasn't long before she pulled out her first fish. "What do I do with it now?" she asked. "Take it off of the hook and put it in that bucket," said Benny. "I'm not touching it," she said. "Well, in that case you have caught your first and last fish," replied Benny. "Manth went to take hold of the mackerel when it started to wriggle on the hook. "Oh noooooo," she said. Then taking a deep breath she grabbed the fish, unhooked it and carefully put it in the bucket. "There's no need to be so careful with them. They will be crab bait in a few minutes," said Ivan. "Are you going to kill the poor thing?" asked Manth. "What do you think we put in the crab and lobster pots as bait?" asked Ivan.

Benny sat there smiling as he pulled fish out of the sea and threw them into the bucket. "I suppose you think it's funny, don't you Benny?"

"Yes, Manth, now catch some more fish."

"My name, in case you have forgotten, is Samantha," said Samantha. "Not any more it's not, now it's Manth. You had better get used to it and start catching some fish. We will soon be at the pots." Benny had to admit his sister was getting quite good at catching the mackerel and not so squeamish about taking them off of the hook and throwing them into the bucket. "We will make a fisherman of you yet, you've done well my girl," said Tom. Ivan shouted to Tom that they were coming up on the first of the lobster pots. Ivan and Benny set about the work of emptying the pots, sorting out what could be kept, what had to be put back and putting in new bait for when they put the pots back in another location later in the morning.

It was proving to be a productive morning with some lovely lobsters and sizeable crabs. Ivan was whistling softly to himself obviously enjoying his work. "Here, Manth, take this and put some bands around its claws," said Ivan, handing her a big lobster. "I'm not touching that thing," she said. "Come on, Manth, it won't hurt you, well not after you have seen to its claws." Ivan placed the lobster into her hands and Benny gave her a hand with the claws. "There, nothing to it," said Ivan with a broad grin on his face. By the time they had emptied all of the pots and set the freshly baited ones it was time for lunch.

Tom took them to one of his secret fishing places, dropped the anchor and started making coffee in the little cabin. Having made the coffee he took out the sandwiches that Dora had made for them all. They sat in the sun watching it sparkle off of the sea's surface, listening to the call of the sea birds and the lapping of the water against the side of the boat, each lost in thoughts of their own. After they had finished their lunch Ivan and Tom baited hooks on fishing lines, each taking a rod and started fishing, two on each side of the boat. Tom showed Manth what to do and she soon got the hang of it even to putting the bait on the hook, but not without some pulled faces and looks of trepidation. Soon Tom landed a fine turbot. "That's unusual, it's getting a bit late in the season for those but welcome all the same." Manth was next with a nice sized brill followed quickly by Tom with another turbot of similar size as the first.

Benny thought his luck was out today when he felt a small tug on the line followed by another, reeling in a john dory just sizeable. Things went quiet for a while when Ivan reeled in a fine haddock of about ten pounds. "That's a lovely fish, Ivan," "said Tom. Benny soon felt his line pulling the rod tip down striking and he hooked into another fish, reeling in another fine haddock only a little smaller than the one Ivan had caught. By the time they left they had quite a haul of various types of fish. Tom was well pleased with all of their efforts and was still smiling to himself as he moored his boat against the harbour wall. Eddie was sitting on the quay waiting for Tom. "How was your day, Tom?"

"We had a good one, Eddie, how about you?"

"Middling, Tom." Is Dora coming down in the van? I've got some fish for her."

"She will be here Dreckly. Are you going to have your smoker going tonight? We caught a couple of nice haddock that I would liked smoked."

"Haddock, Tom? Yes drop them around my place later and I will get them done tonight. Dora can pick them up in the morning. Hey, boy, have you given it any thought about coming out with me?"

"Yes, I've given it some thought and I'll come out with you one day next week and the name's Benny."

"I'll keep you to that," said Eddie.

Just then Dora arrived at the quay in the van to pick up the day's catch. "Looks like you had a pretty good day, Tom," said Dora. "Yes, the fish were biting well today. Eddie has some fish for you to pick up and could you keep the haddock on ice and bring them home with you later? Eddie is going to smoke them tonight, ready for you in the morning. Tomorrow, Ivan and I have a fishing party booked, so we won't be doing our usual stuff. Benny and Manth will have to spend the day with you. Okay?"

"Who is Manth, may I ask? Her name was Samantha when she went out with you this morning."

"She and Ivan had a bit of a dispute about her name. Ivan was going to call her Sam and she got a bit uppity about that as she does. Ivan said he wasn't going to spend his time calling her Samantha, so he said he was going to call her Manth and Manth she has been all day."

"How does Samantha feel about that, may I ask?"

"Well, she doesn't seem to object," said Tom. Tom and Ivan loaded the fish into Dora's van. Tom, Benny and Manth then walked back to the house while Dora went to see Eddie.

Tom went to his workshop while Benny watched him making pieces for his model galleon. Manth went into the house for a shower to get the smell of fish off of her. Dora arrived home later that day, finding Samantha in the lounge watching the T. V. "Samantha, love, how do you feel about being called Manth? I can have a word with the men if it's going to upset you."

"No, it's alright, Aunt Dora, I'm getting used to it now. Don't tell anyone but I quite like it. it's unusual." The following morning after breakfast Manth and Benny climbed aboard the van with Aunt Dora to go firstly to Eddie's house for the smoked haddock, then to the shop. Aunt Dora asked them both if they wanted to help in the shop or go out with Dawn, a lady who delivered fish to the hotels and restaurants who were regular customers of Dora's. They decided to go out with Dawn.

After being introduced to Dawn and Dawn to the twins they loaded the fish orders and climbed back in the van. "Right, let's get this show on the road," said Dawn. The one thing Dora had not told the twins was that Dawn drove the van like she was a rally driver high on Red Bull. They flashed along the narrow lanes with high banks on both side covered in foxgloves and ferns, they slipped in and out of passing places on meeting oncoming vehicles like an eel on ice. At the same time Dawn was singing along with the radio at the top of her voice and if she didn't know the words to the songs she sang some of her own. Manth was white faced and white knuckled holding onto the door handle and anything else she could hold onto. Benny was enjoying the ride and laughing at Dawn's singing. The last call of the day was to a lady in Penzance named Annabelle, an old school friend of Dora's who made various fish pies and fishcakes for sale in Dora's shop.

"So you are Dora's niece and nephew then," said Annabelle. "Yes, this is Benny and I am Manth. We are twins and I am the eldest," said Manth. "That is an interesting name. Where does it come from?" asked Annabelle. "Up until yesterday I was Samantha, I wouldn't be called anything else But I went out on Tom's boat yesterday and Ivan, Tom's crewman, wouldn't call me Samantha and wanted to call me Sam. I don't like Sam so he called me Manth and now they all call me Manth."

"I have the same problem. People want to call me Ann, Anna, Belle, Bella never Annabelle, but I insist on it." After a nice chat Dawn loaded the pies that Annabelle had made and they climbed into the van and headed back to the shop. "Did you enjoy the trip out?" asked Aunt Dora as they walked into the shop. "It was like a ride on the world's best roller coaster," said Benny. "Ah, Dawn's driving. I should have warned you. Still you are both in one piece, that's the main thing.

"What would you like for lunch? What about one of my Cornish pasties. They are the best in Cornwall made by my own fair hand." Manth and Benny both accepted Aunt Dora's offer of a pasty with a cola for Benny and an orange drink for Manth. After lunch they helped out in the shop until it was time to go to the harbour to collect Eddie's Fish.

"Benny my boy, you still coming out with me next week? You can come along as well if you like, Manth," said Eddie. "If they go along with you, Eddie, you look after them like they were your own, no, better than your own, you hear, Eddie?"

"Message understood, Dora. They will come to no harm. They loaded Eddie's fish and returned to the shop. After cleaning the shop at closing time Benny and Manth decided to walk back to Aunt Dora's house. When they got back to the house Tom was in his workshop working on his model ship. "Had a good day, Benny?"

"Not as good as fishing, but Dawn's driving along the narrow lanes is an experience."

"Experience! You can say that again. Lethal is what I call it."

"How did your fishing trip go, Tom?"

"Much as expected. They caught some good fish. One of the boys pulled out a nice conger eel, not a record breaker but nice just the same."

"Are Manth and me coming out with you tomorrow, Tom?"

"If that is what you want to do. Yes. I will give you a call in the morning. Because of the tide we will have to start a bit earlier."

The next morning true to his word Tom came and gave Benny a call. Benny was up, showered and dressed in record time and halfway through his breakfast before Manth made an appearance. "I thought perhaps you had changed your mind about coming today, Manth," said Benny. "I have more to do than you in the morning. My hair takes an age to do, all you do is give yours a rub with a towel. You don't even have to comb it, that's why you have nearly finished your breakfast and I've not started mine."

"Excuses, excuses," said Benny. "Come on the two of you or Tom will have to go without you. The tide won't wait and Tom won't miss it, so get a move on," said Aunt Dora.

Ten minutes later Tom and the twins were walking down to the harbour in the early morning sunlight. As they walked along the quay Eddie's boat passed them on his way out to sea. The twins gave him a wave, and he replied with a toot on the ship's horn. Ivan was busy working when they went aboard Tom's boat. "Are we ready to go?" asked Tom. Ivan replied, All ready, Tom. I'll cast off and we will be on our way." Once they were out of the harbour they increased their speed and headed for the crab and lobster pots the sun glinting off of the calm sea. Reaching the pots, they cut the speed and started lifting the pots. It seemed to Benny that it was about an average catch. When all of the pots had been emptied, Ivan and Benny put new bait in them as fast as Manth could catch the fish to do it and Tom took them to a place they hadn't been to before. Tom said it was his secret place.

Once the pots were placed they made their way to another of Tom's favourite fishing spots where there was a shipwreck on the sea floor. They baited their hooks and dropped the lines overboard and within minutes Manth was fighting with a sizeable cod. She hauled it out of the water with a broad grin on her face. "Is no one else going to catch anything today?" she taunted. Baiting her hook again, she dropped it overboard and before it even reached the bottom she had another fish on the hook. Reeling it in she landed another nice cod. Manth never said a word, but the look on her face told the story. Nobody caught anything for some time. Then Manth caught a nice plaice. "Three nil," she said under her breath. Tom brought out sandwiches and hot coffee from the little cabin. While they were eating lunch Ivan's rod very nearly went overboard. He grabbed it just in time but he had a fight on his hands. He fought for what seemed like an age before he landed a very large Conger eel. Tom looked at the fish. "That's a monster, Ivan. Let's measure it, weigh it, take pictures then put it back." Ivan agreed, so the eel was set free to live another day. A few more fish were caught before it was time to leave and Tom pulled up the anchor and they set off for home.

Perhaps half an hour later Tom looked a little worried, spinning the wheel one way then the other, "What's up, Tom?" asked Ivan. "She's not responding to the wheel. We have no steering. We can't get her home like this."

"Let me take a look," said Benny. "How are you going to do that?" asked Tom. "I'll climb over the side and take a look. I'm a very good swimmer."

"I can't let you do that, Benny, it's too dangerous. We don't know what the current is like out here."

"Have you got any rope, Tom?"

"Yes, why?"

"Tie the rope around my waist. Then I can't get washed away, and you can pull me in at any time." Ivan fetched a long length of rope while Benny took off his shoes and clothes and stood on the deck in his underpants. Tom dropped the anchor and cut the engine. We will give you one minute, then we will pull you in, okay? Benny dropped into the cold clear water, while Ivan kept an eye on the time.

Benny soon found the problem. The rudder was hanging useless, the wood split. Benny swam up to the surface, treading water while telling Tom what the problem was. "Come on out, Benny. I'll see if Eddie is on the radio. If not I'll get the lifeboat to come and tow us back to the harbour."

"Wait a minute, Tom give me a short piece of rope, a sharp knife and a piece of wood about two feet in length. I might be able to make a quick fix."

"No, you come on out."

"Let him have a go, Tom, he is good at fixing things Dad gives him all the broken things to mend and what have we got to lose? Half an hour in time, that's all." Tom relented and fetched the things Benny needed, he handed the rope, knife and wood over to him. "You have one minute, then we pull you up for a breath." Benny dived down and grabbing the rudder he forced it into place. The rope tightened and pulled him to the surface. Benny took a couple of deep breaths, put his thumb up and dived down again. This time he wrapped the rope around the rudder and the post it had broken away from before the rope pulled him to the surface again. Benny again took two deep breaths and dived. He inserted the piece of wood into the rope and tightened by twisting the piece of wood, then tied it in place with a piece of rope to keep it in place. He was pulled to the surface again and after taking a couple of breaths he told Tom to try the wheel. Tom turned the wheel in the cabin and came back with a smile on his face. "Okay, Benny, out you come and dry yourself."

Tom started the engine, pulled up the anchor and they set off for the harbour. Tom phoned Dora asking her or Dawn to meet them at the quayside to take the catch, as the boat would take a day or two to have a new rudder. "How are you getting the boat back to the harbour with no steering?"

"Benny made a quick fix to get us back. He's a clever lad and a good diver."

"Is he alright?" asked Dora. "Yes, he's fine. Are you on your way to the harbour with the van?"

"No, I'm too busy. Dawn will be waiting for you Tom." They pulled into the harbour where Dawn was waiting with the van. "How are you two?" she asked the twins. "Good," replied Manth and Benny. "I hear you have had a bit of trouble today, broken rudder," Dora said."

"Yes, I fixed it enough to get us home, but the boat is going to be out of action for a day or two. Tom is going to put it in the shallows so that he can work on it at low tide. He said that he knows a boatbuilder on the north coast that would have one. All he would have to do is collect it and fit it."

Tom was talking on his phone while Ivan, Manth and Benny loaded the day's catch into the van. Tom finished his phone call and turning to Ivan asked if he would start taking the broken rudder off of the boat tomorrow at low tide. Ivan said that he would. "I will fetch the new rudder tomorrow morning. Benny, what are you going to do tomorrow?"

"I will see if it would be alright to go out with Eddie. He is always asking me to go out on his boat."

"That's a good idea, I'll phone him and see if that would be alright with him."

"What about you, Manth?"

"Could I come with you, Tom? I would like to see some more of Cornwall."

"If that is what you would like to do that's fine with me, and I don't drive like Dawn."

Dawn left for the shop in the van and the rest of them walked out of the harbour for the short walk to the cottage. Tom phoned Eddie to arrange for Benny to go with him in the morning. Benny and Tom went to the workshop, while Manth went to clean the day's grime off in the shower. Benny watched Tom as he worked on the model. Every movement of his hands were precise, making the ship as lifelike as possible. Aunt Dora arrived home in the van and soon called Tom and Benny in for dinner. The talk around the dinner table was all about Benny's diving under the boat to make a quick fix to the rudder rather than call for the lifeboat to tow them back to the harbour. Tom had arranged for the use of a pickup truck for the day to be delivered tomorrow morning.

Morning came. Tom had given Benny a call so that he would be ready when Eddie got to the cottage. Eddie arrived in his Jeep, beeping the horn as he pulled up in front of the cottage. Tom asked Eddie if he had time could he take a look at some of his pots. "Consider it done, Tom and I'll look after the boy like he was my own. Alex, my niece, is coming out with me today, so he will have some company."

"He's a good boy Eddie, good at catching the bait and baiting the pots. He'll pull his weight and be no trouble." Eddie drove off with Benny sitting in front with Eddie. When they reached the harbour Eddie parked in the harbour car park and they walked together to Eddie's boat. As they were climbing aboard, a noisy motorbike pulled up and parked by Eddie's equipment shed. "Here's Alex, noisy little so and so, ain't she?" said Eddie, taking his fingers out of his ears.

"Hello Uncle Eddie," said Alex kissing him on the cheek. "Morning, Alex, hope you are up to doing a day's work, although you have a helpmate. This here is Benny." Benny said hello to Alex, who was climbing out of her motorcycle leathers. "Hello, Benny, it's nice to meet you. Do you live local?"

"No, me and my twin sister Manth are on holiday down here with my Uncle Tom."

"Tom Trevanion, why are you not on his boat?"

"Broken rudder. He and Manth have gone to pick a new one up from a friend of his in Padstow."

"Okay, let's get this show on the road. Cast off, Benny. Benny undid the mooring ropes, gave the boat a push away from the quayside and jumped onboard. Eddie started the engine and they made their way out of the harbour out to the open water. "Do you need some bait catching, Eddie?" asked Benny. "Give him a rod and a bucket, Alex." Benny sat at the back of the boat and started fishing for mackerel and after a few minutes he was putting fish in the bucket.

Alex came and sat beside him, "You have done this before, haven't you?"

"Tom and Ivan taught me a few days ago when we first got down here."

"Where do you live Benny?"

"In Norfolk," replied Benny. "Not too far from the sea then," said Alex. "Just a few miles, Manth and me spend as much time as we can at the beach."

"Time to start work, Alex, pots coming up on the starboard side." Benny kept on fishing and he soon had enough fish in the bucket so he gave Alex a hand with baiting the pots and emptying the pots that Alex was pulling onboard. He measured the crabs and the lobsters and secured their claws like Ivan had shown him. "Well done, young Benny, if you want a job when you are older come down and see me. Now we will go and look at Tom's pots."

Chapter IV

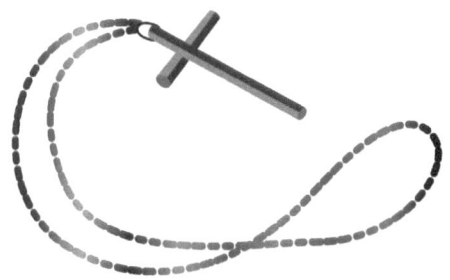

Meanwhile Tom and Manth had climbed into the pickup truck that had been delivered to the cottage by one of Tom's friends. They set off going across country to Padstow. Tom had told her that it was about 46 miles away and would take just over an hour, but as it was the holiday season it might take longer because of the traffic. They made good time, arriving in one hour and twenty minutes, when Tom drove into his friend's boatyard. They both got out of the pickup truck and went in search of Tom's, friend, Martin, whom they found cleaning the hull of a boat ready for painting. "Martin, you old reprobate, how are you? I've not seen you in an age and how's business? You look busy."

"Can't complain, Tom. Not making a fortune but keeping the wolf from the door and who is this lovely young lady you've brought to see me?"

"Manth, this is Martin. Martin, this is Manth my niece."

"Nice to meet you, Manth."

"Likewise," replied Manth.

"You said on the phone you wanted a rudder."

"Yes, the rudder broke away from my old fishing boat yesterday and I need to fix it fast."

"What boat you using these days?"

"The same one you sold me half a lifetime ago."

"Then my friend you are in luck, I just happen to have the very thing. I would have thought you would of got yourself a new boat by now, Tom!"

"Well, Martin, you can't improve on perfection and you built her so you should know."

"Right, let's go and get this rudder for you and load it on your vehicle." They walked back across the boatyard and into a large shed. There leaned against one of the walls was what Tom and Manth had come to Padstow for. "You are a saint, Martin, I thought of all the boatbuilders in Cornwall you had to be favourite being the builder of my boat."

"Just glad to be of help, Tom. You going straight back?"

"No, I thought I would treat Manth to some of Rick Stien's fish and chips. While the tide is still in then I'll help Ivan fix this rudder on the boat and with luck we might get her out again tomorrow. Send me your bill or you can put it on the credit card now, Martin."

"Card, bill, what are you talking about, Tom? Things don't break on the boats I build, and if they wear out they have a lifetime guarantee. There will be no charge and that's final."

Tom and Manth sat in the pickup truck eating fish and chips and drinking coffee on the car park safe from the food-stealing gulls. "Are you ready, Manth? By the time we get back the tide will have turned, so Ivan and I should be able to put this rudder on." It took a little longer to get back home and by the time they got to the harbour Ivan had taken the broken rudder off of the boat. He looked a picture covered from head to toe in stinking grey harbour mud. Manth called and waved to him from the pickup truck and he came squelching over to the truck. "Did you have any luck, Tom?"

"I've got just the thing, in fact it was made for the job." Ivan looked in the back of the pickup. "Hey, that's identical to the one I have just taken off, well I mean before it got broken. How did you manage that Tom?"

"Long story short it came from the man who built the boat. He wouldn't take any payment, saying things he built didn't break and things that wear out have a lifetime guarantee."

"Well, standing here talking isn't going to get this put on the boat, so let's get it fixed so we can go fishing tomorrow."

Tom and Ivan carried the rudder over to the boat, while Manth sat on the bonnet of the truck. Much as she would like to help she wasn't going to roll about in the harbour's mud. Eddie and Benny pulled up in Eddie's jeep and Alex stopped behind on her motorcycle. "Did Tom get a new rudder, Manth?" asked Benny. "Yes, Ivan and Tom are putting it on now. Tom thinks he will have the boat finished and go fishing tomorrow. "Who is your new friend, Benny?" asked Manth. "Sorry, Manth, this is Alex Eddie's niece. Alex, this is my twin sister, Manth."

"Nice to meet you, Manth," said Alex. On seeing Eddie pull up in his jeep, Tom trudged back through the mud to the pickup. Saying hello to Eddie and Alex, he said to Eddie, "Did you get a chance to look at my pots, Eddie?"

"With Benny and Alex along with me we had plenty of time, Tom. They worked their socks off. Your catch and mine are in the jeep. I'll take it over to Dora at the shop."

"How did the boy do, Eddie?"

"I told him if he ever wanted a job to come and see me. It looks like he is born to it!"

"Thanks, Eddie, you are a saint, but I'd better get back and help Ivan. See you tomorrow, mate."

Tom trudged back through the grey stinking mud to help Ivan put the new rudder on the boat. Manth and Benny sat on the pickup for a while watching progress on Tom's boat before walking back to the cottage. At five twenty Aunt Dora came in talking on her phone. Finishing her conversation on the phone she said. "It's just us for dinner. Tom and Ivan are still working, but Tom thinks they will have the rudder on before the water gets too high. That evening Tom walked into the cottage soaking wet. He and Ivan had put the new rudder on the boat as the tide had come in. They had finished the job with the sea water up to their waists, then tested the boat's steering by taking it back to its usual place at the quayside next to Eddie's boat. Tom had then walked back to the cottage, not now covered in the grey stinking mud as the incoming tide had washed most of it off.

Tom came out of the bathroom clean, warm and smelling a lot sweeter than when the twins had last seen him. "Did you get it finished?" asked Benny. "Yes, it's all done and tested, ready for the morning."

"We have had dinner, Tom, what would you like?" asked Aunt Dora. Tom asked, "What did you and the twins have?"

"Steak pie and veggies," answered Dora. "Is there any left?" inquired Tom.

"There is some pie left. I can put it in the microwave. But there are no veggies. I can do you some chips to go with it if you would like that."

"Well, I had some of Rick Stien's chips for lunch with Manth, but you know me, Dora, I can eat chips for breakfast, dinner and tea so that will be fine."

"Are you two coming out with me in the morning or have you had enough of fishing for a while?" asked Tom. "We will be there if you give us a call in the morning," said Benny and Manth.

Morning came wet and windy, the first wet weather Benny and Manth had had since leaving Norfolk. "Are you sure you want to be out on the boat in this weather? It can be cold and it will be choppy once we get out of the harbour," said Tom. They set off walking to the harbour. "I've got some waterproofs on the boat.

They will be a bit on the large side, but you can fold the arms and legs up and they will keep you both dry." When they got onboard Tom took out the waterproofs from a locker. "I keep these onboard for when we hire the boat out for the fishing trips that we do from time to time." Ivan was later than he usually was, but that was probably because he had been talking to Alex on his way past Eddie's boat. Ivan climbed aboard with a smile and water running from his hair onto his face. Tom started the engine and they set off out of the harbour. As Tom had said, the waters soon became choppy and the wind was biting out in the open. Benny and Manth grabbed a fishing rod each and a bucket for the bait fish that they soon were hauling aboard. The cold weather didn't seem to make any difference to the fish.

They soon reached the crab and lobster pots and Ivan pulled them out of the water, Benny emptied them and did the measuring and Manth secured their claws. "Teamwork," said Tom. "I don't know about teamwork, it's more like a well-oiled machine," said Ivan. When all of the pots had been lifted and emptied they re-baited them and set off for another spot a few miles away that Tom sometimes used and returned the pots to the seabed. Tom had been listening to the shipping forecast on the radio and said. "I think we shall call it a day. Things are starting to get a bit stormy and the forecast is for it to get worse, so let's head for home." As they travelled back to the harbour the weather did take a turn for the worse. Tom phoned Dora to say that they had done the pots and were returning to the harbour because of the worsening weather.

Dora didn't say so but she was glad Tom was heading home. She didn't like the idea of the twins being out in the boat in rough weather. It would break her heart if anything should happen to the twins. As they reached the harbour nearly all of the small fishing boats were back in the safety behind the harbour walls and they tied up in the usual place behind Eddie's boat, which Alex and Eddie were just leaving. "Is Dora coming for the fish?" asked Eddie. "No, Dawn is still doing the deliveries."

"Okay, Tom, I'll take the lot in the jeep," said Eddie. Ivan and Alex loaded the fish into the back of the jeep. Then Ivan put on a crash helmet that Alex handed to him, climbed on the back of Alex's motorbike and they noisily roared off out of the harbour. Tom, Manth and Benny took the short walk to the cottage in the rain.

As the evening wore on the wind got stronger, whistling around the gables and the chimney pots, while the trees in the garden were thrashing about as if being shaken by some giant's hand. The rain fell in torrents, filling the gutters and running in streams down the window panes. "Not a night to be out and about nor in anything out at sea," said Tom. In the morning the storm was still raging, perhaps a little less rain but the wind was blowing about 80 miles an hour and there were reports on the television of roofs being destroyed and trees uprooted. "We won't be going out today. It's a day for staying inside and hoping this storm blows itself out by nightfall." The twins spent the day watching the television and Manth wrote in her diary, one of those things she did from time to time.

The day seemed to drag by. Tom, couldn't settle to anything as he was too wound up to work on his model. Dora was at the shop so all there was to do was watch the television or read. Tom and Dora had a bookcase with a variety of books from westerns to murder mystery. Benny picked up one on the history of Cornish towns, villages and traditions. He curled up on the sofa and started reading it and when Dora came home Benny was still on the sofa engrossed in the book. The rain had now stopped, but the wind was still trying to move everything that wasn't nailed down. After dinner Benny went back to reading the Cornish book he had taken out of the bookcase. He had never been a big reader, but this book had fired up his imagination, perhaps because of the references to smugglers, wreckers and mining. Tom said, "I will give you a call in the morning if the wind has abated." Dora handed Manth the phone and said, "Phone your mum and dad and let them know that we are all safe down here." By the time morning had come there was just a stiff breeze, so Tom woke Benny for a day in the boat.

As Tom, Manth and Benny walked towards the harbour there were broken tree branches and debris all over the road. When they reached the harbour it looked like a war zone with small dingies, crab, lobster pots and seaweed in heaps scattered here and there. Tom climbed aboard his boat. It seemed undamaged, as did Eddie's. They both looked a bit weather-beaten, but no real problems. The roar of a motorbike engine took their attention as it stopped at Eddie's boat. Ivan climbed off of the bike and gave Alex the crash helmet he had been wearing. He walked to Tom's boat with a smile on his face, as he climbed aboard softly singing to himself. Every one was smiling, except that is for Manth, who was looking daggers in Alex's direction.

They left the harbour, pushing through floating seaweed that had been washed towards the harbour. They headed out into the choppy open water, the spray sometimes breaking over the bow and giving them all an unwanted shower. When they reached the pots Ivan was still singing softly to himself with a faraway look in his eyes. "Ah, the love bug bites," said Tom. "What?" said Ivan. "Alex," said Tom. "No, we are just old school friends, Tom, nothing more."

"Of course!" said Tom. Having heard this brightened Manth's day. The pots were lifted one by one, but the catch was not as good as it usually was. In fact it was pretty poor. "Let's try our hand at the wreak," said Tom. They all agreed, so they set off for the wreak. Tom made coffee while the rest of them baited hooks and dropped them over the side of the boat and came out of the little cabin carrying coffee and sandwiches for them all.

They all sat eating sandwiches and drinking coffee with little action from the seabed below them. Ivan, having finished his lunch went back to singing to himself. It might have been annoying but for the fact that he had quite a good singing voice. But his voice could not charm the fish onto the hooks. Tom was the first to catch a fish, but it was a dogfish and not worth keeping, so it went back over the side to live another day. After another hour Tom said, "Let's call it a day," so they returned back to the harbour. When they secured the boat to the quay Tom climbed up the steel ladder to the top, as it was still low tide. He dropped a rope down to the boat, Ivan put the meagre catch into a plastic tray and tied the rope to it and Tom hauled it onto the quayside while the others climbed up the ladder. "We can manage this fish, Ivan you can get off home. Me and the twins will carry it to the shop. See you in the morning."

The three of then walked to Dora's shop. She was surprised to see them so early and said, "What's wrong, Tom?"

"Nothing, Dora, except it's been a waste of time being out there today."

"What are you going to do for the rest of the day?" Dora asked. Tom answered, "I'll be in the workshop if you need me for anything."

"What about the twins?" asked Dora. Benny said, "I have a book to finish reading." Manth said, "I'll stay here with you, Aunt Dora."

"Right, Tom, I'll see you at home later." Tom and Benny walked back to the cottage, where Tom went into his workshop and Benny settled on the sofa with the book he had been reading. He was so engrossed in it that he never heard Aunt Dora and Manth come home. Dora asked Tom to help her get dinner ready, which was a change from the usual. Dora didn't always like Tom helping in the kitchen.

After dinner Dora said to the twins "Tom and I have had a chat. You have been down here for a week or more and all that you have done is work. That's not a holiday, so tomorrow we are going shopping. We want to get you both a wetsuit each with flippers, snorkel and mask. There is a lovely little cove a short walk from here, where you can watch the underwater life. It's called Frenchy's cove.

In the morning after breakfast Tom and Dora took them into Penzance to get them kitted out for their snorkelling adventures. Tom and Dora seemed to know every shopkeeper in the town and came away with some bargains. Then they went down a side street for lunch in a little cafe who was one of Dora's customers. After lunch they took in the sights of the town and bought new swimwear. Benny was very interested in the town, having read about it in the book he was reading. They walked around all of the main shopping areas, peering in shop windows, Tom looking in the second-hand shops for anything he could use in his model making. All too soon it was time to return to the cottage and dinner. The twins put their purchases in their bedrooms ready for use. It was agreed at dinner that tomorrow, depending on the weather, the twins would spend the day at Frenchy's cove.

Morning came promising to be hot and sunny, so the twins were going to Frenchy's cove. "Just a word of warning, at one end of the cove is Rockfall point. Stay clear of it. The rip tides and currents are unpredictable and the rocks unstable, but the rest of the cove is a lovely place to spend a sunny day," said Tom. Aunt

Dora made them a packed lunch with cold drinks in a cool box. The twins changed into the new wet suits, putting the masks, flippers, snorkels and towels into backpacks and picked up the cool box, saying. "Goodbye," to Aunt Dora and headed for Frenchy's cove a short walk away.

Chapter V

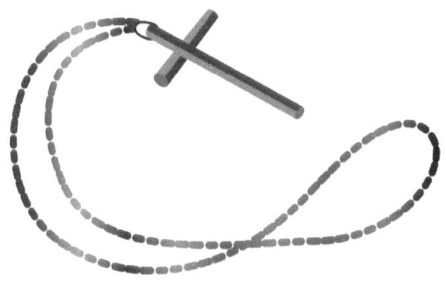

The twins walked out onto the soft sand of the cove, the blue water sparkling invitingly in the warm morning air. Manth found a place she liked and put down her backpack. Benny followed suit, taking out the towel from his backpack and spreading it out on the sand. Then he took out the mask, flippers and snorkel and, taking off his sandals, walked down the beach to dip his toes into the little ripples of salt water that raced up the sand. "Come on, Manth, the waters fine he shouted to his sister. Benny put on the flippers and spit in the mask, rubbing it all around the glass like the chap in the shop had told him to do, to stop it misting up. Then he dipped the mask in the water, put the rubber strap around his head and adjusted it, finally pushing the snorkel tube between his head and the strap.

Benny soon found out it was easier to walk backwards when wearing flippers than forwards. When the water was halfway up his legs he turned around, put the mouthpiece of the snorkel in his mouth and dived into the water. Just relaxing and kicking with his legs he moved through the water with hardly any effort, taking in the sights beneath the small waves. After a few minutes Manth joined him with her facemask steamed up. Benny said, "Didn't you spit in the mask and rub it in?"

"NO I DID NOT," she replied. Whilst treading water Benny took her mask off of her face, spit on the glass, rubbed it all over, dipped the mask in the water and gave it back. She put the facemask back on and swam alongside Benny, venturing into deeper water and coming across some plants that looked like grass growing from the seabed. Manth tapped Benny on the arm and pointed into the grass. There hiding in the grass were two seahorses.

After about two hours of seeing small fish, crabs and other creatures, Benny was feeling hungry. He tapped Manth on the arm and pointed to the shore. He climbed out of the water. The sun was beginning to feel hot as he took off his flippers and walked up the beach. He sat on his towel and took out his lunch and a cold drink from the cool box. He sat there enjoying his lunch in the sunshine, watching as Manth headed back to the shore. His thoughts drifted to Tom and Ivan out there somewhere on the boat earning a living catching the fish for Dora's shop. Manth flopped down on her towel. "Nice here, Benny, isn't it?"

"Yes, I wonder why it's called Frenchy's cove, sort of a strange name for a place in Cornwall isn't it? I'll ask Tom when he has finished work later. About an hour later Benny walked back down to the water and getting his snorkelling gear back on, dived back into the water. Veering off to his left to see if the seabed was any different there, he came across a small rocky outcrop. He guessed the water was about three fathoms deep. Stopping above the rocks, he watched and soon saw a small lobster and a brown crab.

Manth joined him a little later, but Benny swam out a little further, coming across another patch of the sea grass. He lay still on the surface of the water watching a small school of little fish swimming in and out of the grass. Manth came up to him but she must have frightened them, for they all darted into the sea grass, hiding amidst their leaves. They stayed in the water for another hour or so, then made their way back to the beach, where they lay on their towels warming in the afternoon sun. When they had both warmed up they packed away the snorkelling equipment and towels into their backpacks, picked up the cool box and headed back to the cottage. As they approached the cottage Benny could see that Tom was working in the workshop. Benny went into the workshop while Manth headed indoors for a shower. "Did you have a nice day at the beach, Benny?" asked Tom. "It was smashing, Tom, thanks for getting us the snorkelling gear. We enjoyed looking at the sea creatures."

"Tom have you any idea why the cove is called Frenchy's cove? It seems a funny name for a cove in Cornwall."

"Sorry, I can't help you there, Benny. My father and grandfather called it that. As far as I know it has always been Frenchy's cove."

"Thanks, Tom, I'll ask Aunt Dora if I can use the

computer after dinner. There might be something on the internet."

"I'm sure that will be alright, Benny. Benny went into the cottage, had a shower and then sat down with his book.

After dinner Benny asked Aunt Dora if he could use her computer, "Of course, Benny, what are you looking for?"

"I'm interested in finding out why Frenchy's cove is so called."

"Help yourself, Benny. I will put the password in for you and you can spend the evening on there if that is what you want to do." Benny searched the internet without much luck, but Benny wasn't going to be put off that quickly. The weather forecast for the following day was hot, so the twins decided to forgo a day on Tom's boat and spend the day snorkelling at Frenchy's cove again. So in the morning the twins set off for the beach with all of their equipment in their backpacks and carrying the cool box. They spread their towels out in the same place as the previous day. It didn't take them long to get into the water, Manth even spitting into her snorkelling mask. They set off looking to see if the seahorses were still where they were yesterday in amongst the seagrass.

It didn't take them long to find them anchored to the seagrass Then they set off towards the edge of the cove on their left. They hadn't looked at that part of the cove yesterday. The sand on the seafloor gave way to rocks with bigger fish and more abundant sea life. Like yesterday they spent an hour or two before returning to the beach for lunch and warming up in the sunshine. When he had finished his lunch Benny sat on his towel watching the boats going to and from the harbour, on the other side of Rockfall point that jutted out into the English Channel. Benny could only guess as to why it had that name, like the village where the cottage was situated, Yarran's Shop. Benny surmised that someone years ago named Yarran had a shop there. What other explanation could there be?

After a while Benny was tired of watching the boats so asked Manth if she was going back into the water. Manth, who had been half asleep, said that she was ready. They put on their snorkelling kit and waded into the sea. They just kicked with their legs slowly and watched as the seabed pass by pointing out things of interest as they came into sight. They had swum out further than they had realized and didn't notice that the current was pushing them towards Rockfall point, the very place that Tom had said to stay away from. Benny was first to notice that the seabed was strewn with boulders and rocks, rocks that were not part of the bedrock.

Benny stopped swimming and treading water and looked around at where they were exactly. He took his mouthpiece out and tapping Manth on the shoulder said, "I think we had better go back." This proved to be more difficult than either of them had imagined, as the current was strong, dragging them towards the open water. They were only a few yards away from the end of Rockfall point. Kicking hard and using his arms, he grabbed the rocky end of the point, then grabbed his sister as she was pulled past him by the current. They hauled themselves out of the water and sat breathing hard on the granite rocks. Benny took off his flippers and started to make his way back to the beach. He had only gone a few feet when something in the rocks caught his attention, in the water wedged between the rocks, bright and shining.

Benny put on his snorkel and mask and tried to reach this shining object, but his hand was too big to reach it. "Manth, see if you can reach down there and get that shining thing. My hand is too big." Manth put her mask and snorkel on and plunged her hand down towards the object, but like Benny her hand was too big to reach into the small crevice and retrieve it. "It's no use, Benny, my hand is too big to get it. What do you think it is anyway?"

"It looks like a coin or a medal of some kind. Do you think we will be able to find this spot again tomorrow, Manth?"

Manth said, "We can make a mound out of some of those loose rocks over there," pointing to some largish boulders."

"Right, I'll bring some over and pile them up and hope the tide doesn't sweep them away in the night." Benny carried the biggest boulders he could manage and built a pile to mark the spot.

Benny and Manth clambered over the rocky point to where the beach met the rocks, then they climbed down onto the sand and walked back to their towels. "How are you going to get whatever it is out of that crevice, Benny?"

"I'll make something in Tom's workshop when we get back, something like one of those litter pickers only smaller."

"Yes that might work, I just hope it's worth all of the effort, that's all." They packed their belonging's into their backpacks, picked up the cool box and walked the short distance back to the cottage. Tom was in the workshop when they arrived at the cottage, "Hi, Tom, had a good day?" asked Benny. "Average, Benny, didn't earn a fortune but enough to keep the wolf from the door. You are not going to ask me loads of questions again that I can't answer, are you Benny?"

"No, Tom, just one, can I use your workshop and tools after dinner? I need to make a gadget."

"Feel free, Benny, fill your boots, my boy.

After dinner Benny went out into the workshop and rummaged around. He found a piece of aluminium tube that looked like a piece of TV aerial He set to work hammering, sawing and drilling and after some time Benny had fashioned something like a litter picker, but with much smaller jaws. To operate it there were two cords, one for opening the jaws and one for closing them. Benny then spent some time picking up things from the workshop floor and when he was happy with his ability he went into the cottage and started to read his book again. In the morning after breakfast, Manth and Benny carried their equipment and walked down to the beach, but instead of remaining on the sand they climbed up the rocks of Rockfall point. They made their way to where they thought they had made a mound of rocks and sure enough they were still in place. Benny peered into the water. The thing that was shining there yesterday was still there in the small crevice.

Benny put on his mask and snorkel, made himself comfortable, dipped his head into the water and reaching in with his new-made tool he guided it into the crevice. After a few failed attempts, Benny managed to grip the item and manoeuvre it out of the crevice. As he lifted the tool it was caught in something else that looked like a thin chain. He put his hand into the water and grabbed the shining thing from between the jaws. He gave the item to Manth and returned to the task of the thin chain. It looked very delicate, so he didn't want to put too much strain on it. After a while he could see that it was joined to something wedged in the crevice. He managed to grab the thing and turn it around so that it would come up through the crevice. With a bit of twisting and turning he brought it clear of the water. It was a cross, maybe four inches long by two and a half inches wide. It was made of what looked like gold and it had five stones, one on each of the legs close to the tips and a bigger one in the middle of the cross. But most striking were the four green stones that were long and thin pointing out from the centre, three the same size and a longer one making a green cross.

Manth was sat on a rock holding the shining thing between her fingers with her mouth wide open. "What's the matter, Manth, are you alright?"

"It, it's gold Benny, Gold!!"

"If you think that's nice, Manth take a look at this," he said, holding up the most beautiful big gold and emerald cross on a gold chain. Manth held out her hand and took the cross from Benny, giving him the gold coin. "Benny, did you look at the back of this cross?"

"No why?"

"There is writing on the back. I think it is Spanish with a date." She rubbed the back with her fingers and it didn't take much to rub the grime off of it. "It says A D 1683."

"How do you think they got here?" asked Manth. Benny shook his head, saying "I haven't a clue, but we are going to find out, Manth. There are a lot of other things that need answers too. Like why is this called Frenchy's cove? Why call this Rockfall point? We are going to go detective and get some answers," said Benny.

First thing they had to do is take their treasure, which had to be put away safely until Tom and Aunt Dora were both home, back at the cottage. It would be pointless telling Tom first and then Aunt Dora afterwards. It would be best to do it after dinner when they were all altogether in the kitchen. Benny and Manth couldn't settle so they went back to the beach without their wetsuits and snorkelling gear, just taking the cool box, towels and swimwear. They lay on their towels and sunbathed, occasionally going for a dip in the sea. The day seemed to drag by, time going by slowly, but the time came to go back to the cottage. Tom was in the workshop and Aunt Dora was in the kitchen preparing dinner. "Had a good day?" asked Aunt Dora. "Smashing," replied Manth.

When dinner was finished Benny said, "We have something to show you both but don't quite know what to do about it. Yesterday, we snorkelled out into the cove a little further than we usually do. Anyway I noticed that the seafloor was different, littered with boulders, not bedrock but ones that had fallen there. When I looked up I could see that the current had taken us across the cove and we were very close to Rockfall point. I grabbed Manth by the arm and a rock on the point and we climbed up onto the point and started walking back. I hadn't taken more than a couple of steps when something bright caught my eye. It was below the water, but neither Manth or I could reach it. It was in a crevice too small to get our hands in.

We marked the spot and came back to the cottage, where I asked if I could use your workshop and tools."

"That's right, I thought you were going to ask me a lot of questions questions that I didn't have the answer to," said Tom. "I needed to make a tool to reach into the crevice, so I made a thing like a litter picker but smaller. This morning we went back to the place we had marked and there in the water still shining was the item. I managed to get hold of it and started lifting it out, but I had caught some sort of a thin chain as well. I reached down and grabbed the shiny item and gave it to Manth without looking at it. I kept a hold of the other thing. It was wedged in the crevice, but using the tool I had made, I managed to turn it around and lift it out."

"So what have you found?" asked Tom. "I'll go and fetch it and show you." Benny went up to his bedroom, took the items from their hiding place and returned to the kitchen. Sitting back down at the table, he put the two items on the table in front of Tom.

Tom picked up the gold coin and let out a low whistle, while Aunt Dora picked up the cross. "It's absolutely beautiful," she said, turning it over in her hand. Tom and Dora exchanged items, looking them over. Tom said, "There is some writing on the back of this but it isn't in English." Manth said "I think it is Spanish, but I'm not sure." Dora went and got her computer. "We will soon find out," she said. She soon found a web page to translate Spanish to English and typed in what was written on the back of the cross, Rosa Maria Dolores my fine granddaughter 1683. Dora put the name into the computer along with the date. There were a lot of Rosa Maria Dolores's that popped up, but only one close to the date. There was a lady of that name, who was a favourite of the king of Spain's court, who went to Mexico early in the 1680's. Her grand-father was a Spanish envoy in Jamaica and also a talented jeweller. She was never seen again.

"Well, that seems to be whose cross you have, but what is it doing in a small cove in Cornwall is anybody's guess," said Tom. "Do we have to give it to the government, or can we keep it?" asked Manth. "I will ask the harbour master. I have his phone number." Tom came back a few minutes later saying. "The harbour master was unsure, as no one would know if it was a shipwreck, or if someone in the dim and distant past had just lost it. He did, however, say that found treasure has to be notified to the local coroner within fourteen days."

"Well, I suppose the first thing is to find out if it is real or fake. I think we all know that it's real, but we are not experts, so let's take it to a jeweller's in Penzance tomorrow afternoon. I think the coin is a Spanish escudo."

When Tom had finished work the next day they went into Penzance, parked the car and went into a fine jeweller's. "Can I help you, sir?" said the man behind the counter. "Do you do valuations?" asked Tom. "I do, what is it that you want valued?" Tom took the cross out of his pocket, unwrapped it and put it on the counter. The jeweller nearly fainted. "Where did you get this?" he asked. "It doesn't matter where it came from, I've got to report it to the coroner in a few days time. I need to know its estimated worth and what the stones are."

"Ah, treasure, well let me look. He turned it over and took out his eyepiece, "Spanish 1683."

"Probably not," said Tom. "What do you mean? it quite clearly says 1683 and the script is Spanish."

"So it might, but the jeweller is a man named Dolores who lived in Jamaica in 1683."

"Sorry, I assumed with the Spanish script it came from Spain."

"Right, it is gold of course. The five stones are, yellow diamonds. I have never come across diamonds like these, beautifully cut with no flaws, quality of the highest. The emeralds are again quite exquisite." He took out his eyepiece, and looked at Tom. "Sir, you have made my day, no you have made my year. As you know, who the jeweller is and where and when it was made puts the value up. I would say it would in today's market make a five-or six-figure sum."

"Thank you," said Tom "have a pleasant day."

"Keep it safe," said the jeweller. Tom wrapped it back up put it in his pocket and he and the twins left the shop.

When they got back to the car Tom said, "We had better take these things to the coroner's office, it's only a stones throw away. I don't like the idea of keeping it at home. Let someone else have the worry. Is that alright with you two? After all they are yours, you found them." The twins agreed. They drove to the coroner's office, parked in the car park, entered the building and went up to the receptionist, a dark haired woman of about 30 years of age. "What can I help you with?"

"We would like to see the coroner."

"In connection with what?" she asked. Tom, looking all around to make sure they weren't being overseen, took the cross and the coin out of his pocket and put them on the desk. "This," he said." She gasped, picked up the phone and said, "I think you had better come out here, Peter."

The coroner came out to the reception straight away. "What is the matter, Cath?" The woman pointed at the two items on the desk without saying a word. The coroner took one look at the items and said, "You had better follow me." He took them to an office and said, "Please come in." There were only two chairs, so he went and came back with two more. "Okay, I guess this is found treasure, is that right? There are some forms to fill in." Tom thought I guessed as much but said nothing. The coroner opened a filing cabinet and took out some forms, "Okay, name of finder."

"Tom said, "Benny and Manth, that is Samantha Franks."

"Where were the items found?" "Rockfall point." "Where exactly is Rockfall point?"

"Between Yarran's Shop and Frenchy's cove," said Tom.

"Address of finder, finders?" Manth gave him the address in Norfolk. "Have you an address here in Cornwall?" Tom gave him his address. "Description of item(s), I'll take photographs, it's easier. Right, that's all for now. I will be in touch."

"Benny said," Can we take some photos now before we go?"

"Of course."

"Tom, could you use the camera on your phone?" Tom took photos from all angles of both of the items. "Thanks, Tom," said Benny.

Tom, Manth and Benny returned home from Penzance. Dora was already preparing dinner when they walked into the cottage. "How did you get on?" She asked. "Well, the jeweller said the cross could be worth a five-or-six figure sum, but we didn't show him the coin. We can find that out on the net. We took some photos we can put them on the computer later. Then we took the things to the coroner, as I didn't want things worth that much money in the house. Let someone else have the worry." After dinner they got the computer fired up and started searching the web for the gold coin. It looked like a 100 escudo piece. If this was what it was it would be worth a fortune. The twins asked Tom if they could go out on the boat in the morning. "Fed up with being treasure hunters already are we?" he asked with a smile. Before going to bed Benny used Aunt Dora's phone to call home and talked to his mum for a few minutes about this and that, then told her about their find on Rockfall point. "It's worth a fortune, mum, we have taken it to the coroner, "Okay, let me talk to your Aunt Dora, please." Benny gave the phone to his aunt. "It's mum," he said.

Tom got Benny and Manth up in the morning. It was another bright day, not scorching hot but nicely warm. Having had breakfast they walked the short distance to the harbour. Ivan was already there talking to Alex. He had a crash helmet in his hand, so it appeared that Alex had given him a lift on the noisy motorbike. Ivan climbed aboard the boat saying good morning to Tom and asking Benny and Manth if they had enjoyed their days off. They both replied that they had. "Good, perhaps you could catch some bait if you still remember how to do it then." Manth got two fishing rods and Benny got a bucket. They waved to Eddie and Alex as they passed them on their way out of the harbour. Benny and Manth were soon hooking into some small fish that they hadn't caught before. "Tom, are these any good?" asked Benny. Tom looked at the fish. "Yes they are herring," said Tom. Benny and Manth kept catching fish and putting them in the bucket. When they got to the crab and lobster pots Benny and Manth emptied the pots that Ivan pulled out of the water, measuring the catch and keeping the sizeable ones and putting the others back. The catch had been a good one so Aunt Dora would have a good day as well.

Ivan came and sat beside them when all of the pots had been emptied and they were on their way to put out more pots in one of Tom's favourite places. "What were you doing for the last few days?" asked Ivan. "Oh just snorkelling in Frenchy's cove," replied Manth. "Did you see anything interesting?"

"Yes, but on the point rather than in the cove," said Benny. "I didn't think there was anything interesting on that old pile of rock," said Ivan. "Depends on where you look, I suppose. Do you know why it's called Rockfall point and Frenchy's cove?" asked Benny. Never learned anything at school about it, so no, sorry, why do you ask?"

"Oh, just interested," said Benny. When they had got back to the harbour and the fish loaded onto Dora's van, Benny said to Manth, "I have something to do. I'll catch you later." Benny walked up into the village and seeing the church tower he headed in that direction.

Benny strolled through the church gate and started looking at all of the headstones, not taking a lot of notice of the newer ones, but studying the older ones. It had taken him longer than he thought it would. He was about to give up when he noticed a headstone close to the church wall and under a large yew tree. He crossed the churchyard to the headstone, which was old and had gone green from the tree but had been protected from most of the weather by its position against the wall. Benny couldn't read the writing, but tracing the letters and numbers with his fingers he thought that perhaps this was what he was looking for. He left the church and walked back to the cottage. Tom said, "Get done what you wanted, Benny?"

"Well, I'm not sure, but I will know more tomorrow if you don't mind me and perhaps Manth not coming out with you again tomorrow."

"Benny, my boy, it's your holiday, you don't have to come out on the boat every day. Do as you please with your days. Tell me, though is it to do with the items you and Manth found?"

"Well kind of. The names of the cove and the point are sort of alien to Cornwall and the items came from thousands of miles away. Perhaps a Spanish coin, a cross made in Jamaica and a cove named Frenchy's cove are all related in some way."

"Well, good luck with that one, Benny." At that moment Manth told them that dinner was ready.

"Manth, do you want to go out on the boat tomorrow?" asked Benny. "Why, what are you planning to do?"

"There is a headstone that I found in the

churchyard. It needs a scrubbing but it's old. I traced the numbers with my fingers and I think it is 1683."

"So we are going to go and scrub a tombstone in the churchyard, to see what is written on it!!"

"Well, yes, that is my plan."

"So the choice is another day's fishing, or scrubbing a headstone."

"No, you can go snorkelling if you want."

"Well, let's go and look at this old tombstone and hope it helps with the mystery." The twins didn't have to get up early in the morning to do what they had planned for the day. Aunt Dora gave them breakfast before going off to her shop. "What are you two doing with yourselves today, then?" asked Aunt Dora. "We are going to the churchyard to scrub an old tombstone to see what the inscription is," replied Manth. "Don't get damaging anything and getting into trouble, will you?"

"No, we are just using soap and water and a bit of elbow grease with a scrubbing brush if we can borrow yours," said Benny. "There is one under the sink along with a bucket if you need one."

"Smashing," replied Benny.

When they had finished their breakfast, with soap, scrubbing brush and a bucket they set off for the churchyard. Benny found the tap and filled the bucket with water before they set off for the headstone. Benny pointed out the stone by the church wall. "It's filthy, we'll never get that clean," said Manth. "We have got to try," said Benny. Benny started scrubbing and it wasn't as hard as he had first thought. After an hour or so and a good few buckets of water and plenty of soap they had cleaned away the dirt and muck that standing in the churchyard over the years had accumulated on the tombstone. Giving it a final rinse with clean water, Benny and Manth bent down and read what was now revealed upon the stone. It said, "Thank you for the second chance in life, Frenchy, 1683."

The twins couldn't believe what they were seeing. It brought more questions than answers, but it did bring the year and Frenchy's cove sort of together. They were just about to walk away, pleased with themselves, when the preacher asked what they were doing in his churchyard. "Benny said, "we were cleaning that headstone," pointing to a very clean headstone. "I can see that, but why?" asked the preacher. "We can't tell you everything, but it has to do with why Frenchy's cove is called that, and why does that headstone have that inscription on it." The preacher bent down and read what was written on it. "I never knew that stone was that old or who Frenchy was. I can also see the connection between the headstone and the cove. Where do the two of you live?" asked the preacher. "We live in Norfolk, but we are on holiday, staying with our Aunt Dora and Uncle Tom at the cottage," said Manth." "How I wonder does it take two strangers from Norfolk to unearth something like this down here in Cornwall?" mused the priest.

"Like I said, we can't tell you everything but we really want to know who Frenchy was and who put this headstone here, for it wasn't Frenchy himself," said Benny. "Quite so, quite so," said the bemused preacher. "Come with me. Perhaps I can shed some light on the subject."

Chapter VI

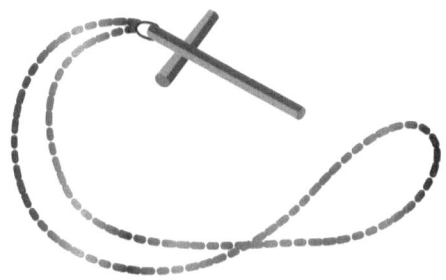

The preacher took them into the church and said, "we have most of the church records going back hundreds of years. Perhaps we can discover some of what you want to know. What are your names?" he asked. "I am Benny Franks. This is my twin sister Manth, that is to say Samantha Franks. She is the eldest." I am Simon, Simon Drinkworthy, Vicar of this parish. Right, let's find those records and have a look to see if we can clear up some of this mystery. Okay, let's go to the rectory. It will be more comfortable than in this chilly church," said Simon with an armful of old books. They followed him to the rectory a short distance away and sitting at his kitchen table they went through the books until they found the records for 1683.

They looked through all of the months until they came to September. There on the 21st was a burial of an unknown man. "Okay, so now we know that this man known as Frenchy by someone, was interred in the churchyard on 21-9-1683," said Manth. Simon was looking through the old record books when he took out a loose folded piece of paper. After reading it he said,

"This might be of interest to you both." He handed it to Manth, who looked at it and slowly made out what it said. It was difficult because of the language. "What does it say, Manth?"

"It's a letter asking for permission to have a headstone erected on an unmarked grave." "Who asked for it?"

"You are not going to believe this, Benny. It was by someone named Abe Trevanion in August 1684."

"Does that name ring a bell? asked Simon. "Our uncle and aunt have that name and as far as we know Uncle Tom's family have lived here for years," said Manth. Simon suggested, "It might be worth your uncle going through his family tree. It is quite easy on the internet these days. There are lots of old documents in the church that haven't been looked at for hundreds of years. I will brush the dust off and have a look to see if any of it in some way relates to your search."

"Thanks, Simon," said Benny. The twins walked back to the churchyard and recovered their bucket and scrubbing brush. Then they walked back to the cottage. Benny's mind was going over what they knew. There was a grave in the churchyard with the name Frenchy, there was a cove called Frenchy's cove. What if anything did they have to do with each other? The date on the grave was 1683 and the same date is on the gold cross they found on Rockfall point. Is it just coincidence or have they somehow got something in common? Lastly, the name Trevanion, their uncle's name and the name on the piece of paper at the church.

At dinner Tom and Dora asked how their day had gone. Manth explained all that they had found out, but it was like a jigsaw puzzle with a lot of the pieces missing. Tom was interested in the fact that his name and the person who put the headstone on the grave, were the same. Dora got the computer out and Tom started tracing his family back through the ages. The first part was easy. His mother and father were both killed in an avalanche whilst skiing in the alps half a dozen years ago. He also knew his grandfather's date of birth and when he had died. The internet site was very helpful. Soon he found his great grandfather, also his great, great grandfather, all of whom had all lived locally and were all fishermen. The computer soon found another relative one more generation back. His family tree was all on the screen for him to see. The twins had decided to go into Penzance the next day to go to the library and see how far back the local paper's records went. Aunt Dora said that the twins could go with Dawn in the morning and she would drop them off in Penzance. They could then catch the bus back in the afternoon. "Thank you, Aunt Dora, that would be very helpful." said Manth.

The next morning the twins were all fired up for the day in Penzance as they jumped in the van with Aunt Dora and headed to the shop. When they had loaded all of the deliveries Dawn climbed in and said, "Penzance, here we come, ready or not." The twins held on tight as Dawn flashed along the narrow country lanes, seemingly oblivious to the oncoming traffic. In no time she dropped the twins off at the local paper. They went into the paper's offices. Finding the receptionist, Manth told her what they required and asked if the paper could help in any way. She phoned someone and after putting the phone down said, "Take a seat. Joe from records will be with you in a minute or two. Perhaps five minutes later Joe turned up. He must have been 70 years of age with a kindly face.

"What can I do for you young people?" he asked. Benny and Manth explained about the cove, the point, the grave in the churchyard and lastly the cross and coin. "Interesting, we may be able to help you. Come with me." He led them into an office where a woman of about forty with striking red hair sat in a large swivel chair. Susan said, "Joe, what can I do for you?"

"Susan, sorry to disturb you, but I thought you might be interested in what these two young persons are here for. He went on to tell Susan what the twins had told him. Her eyebrows rose at the word treasure. Susan looked at the twins. "Where do you come from?" Manth told her that they were on holiday from Norfolk and were staying with their aunt and uncle in Yarran's Shop. "I wonder if in return for helping you, could we run a story?" Benny said, "If you keep the location secret, yes. You might want to phone Uncle Tom. He has some pictures on his phone he could send to you." Benny gave Susan the number.

Susan said "Joe, take them down to the records office and see what you can dig up." Joe with the twins in tow went down the stairs to the records office in the basement. "What was the year you are interested in?"

"1683," answered Benny. Joe went to work firstly on

the computer. His fingers flying across the keyboard and with an occasional nod of the head or an oomph, then he got up and looked in some old looking files that were in an old filing cabinet. We don't have much on the year 1683. There was no paper back then, just a news sheet that was issued once a week, we believe. But there is one thing, it seems that there was a great storm that lasted for three days that caused floods and landslides. He went back to the computer working the keys like a hacker, then he pointed to something on the screen.

This he said was written some years later. It is about a place called "The Beak." It seems this was a large rock overhanging a large cave. After that storm the overhang and the cave had disappeared. There was, it was said at the time, a landslide, but there is no evidence to support it. This may be or not be your Rockfall point, I shall keep searching all of our files and some of the county records and see what we can discover." With that he took the twins back to see Susan. Susan was looking at some photographs on her phone." Joe, take a look at these," they were the photo's that Tom had sent. "Are those the things that you found on Rockfall point?" he asked. "Yes, replied Benny. "Well, they didn't swim over here by themselves, so something happened between 1683 and when you found them a few days ago."

"Okay, we will run a story but keep the location secret. I've checked with your Uncle Tom and we will send a reporter around this evening to write it up. These two items must be worth a fortune. Where are they now may I ask?"

"With the coroner, and you are right a fortune!!" answered Manth.

They left Joe and Susan and went in search of the museum. The museum proved to be a non-starter, so they went for lunch before catching the bus for home. While they were having lunch Manth asked Benny if he thought that The Beak and Rockfall point were the same place. "You saw the boulders on the seafloor. Do they look like the rough granite we climbed on, on the point?"

"So you think there was a landslide?"

"I think that it is possible, Manth. They finished their lunch and walked to the bus stop, catching the bus ten minutes later. They both were in their own thoughts for the trip home. When the got to the cottage Tom was already at home and asked, "How did your day go?"

"The paper was helpful but the museum was a waste of time," replied Manth. "Did the paper get the pictures alright? I never know with these electronic gadgets."

Benny replied, "Yes, Susan did get them. She was well impressed, so someone is coming around after dinner tonight."

"Did you learn anything new?" asked Tom.

"Well, it seems that there was a place called The Beak and during 1683 there was a storm that lasted for three whole days. When the storm had passed The Beak was gone and no one seems to know exactly where it was. The thing is the cross has the date on it, 1683. The

Beak disappeared in 1683 and we found the cross on Rockfall point. Is Rockfall point The Beak?" said Benny. "That is a good point," said Tom. When dinner was finished and the dishes washed and put away the front doorbell rang. Tom went to the door where a voice said. Hello, my name is Susanna Wainwright. Call me Susan. I take it you are Tom? We spoke on the phone."

"Yes, please come in. We are all in the kitchen, is that alright?" Tom introduced Susan to Dora and Dora to Susan. "We were expecting a reporter, not the editor of the Penzance Recorder," said Tom. "This story has caught my imagination. It is obviously very, very difficult trying to confirm facts that happened such a long time ago. But it is probably written down somewhere, it's just a matter of unearthing. Perhaps a story in the paper might jog someone's memory, a memory of something they have seen, heard or read about.

"Now Tom, as I understand it your name is Trevanion, the same name as on a piece of paper found in the local church records by the Rev. Simon Drinkworthy. That a man applied to have a headstone erected on an unmarked grave of a man found drowned on the beach in 1683. The name Frenchy is on that headstone. Whether that was his name or his origin is not known. If that person whose name is on that paper was a relative of yours it would be ten generations back. Tracing your family history back ten generations is not impossible and we will help you do that. It would be a strange coincidence if it turned out to be one of your kinfolk. We will concentrate on that aspect first, then we will look at trying to find out if The Beak and Rockfall point are one and the same places among other things. Thank you all for all of the information you have given the Recorder, we will be in touch soon. This is an enigma we intend to solve." With that Susan bade them all a very good evening. Tom took her to the door and she stepped out into the cool evening air.

Two days later Tom got a call on his boat from Susan, asking if she could call around to the cottage that evening, as there had been some progress on his ancestry. Tom said he would be delighted to see her later that day. Susan arrived a little after half past six ringing the doorbell. She was shown into the kitchen again. "Would you like a coffee or tea?" asked Dora. "We were just about to have one."

"Coffee would be nice, no milk or sugar thanks." While Dora was making coffee Susan took out some documents from her battered old briefcase and spread them out on the kitchen table.

"This is what we know so far, On one large sheet of paper was Tom's family tree. "This is what we know so far Right, bottom line is you Tom, your date of birth and the date of your marriage to Dora. Next line up is your parents, your dad's date of birth and marriage. Each line going up is your father's father, and his father's father. If you look at the line before the top you will see an Abe Trevanion. Abe being short for Abraham. We are pretty certain that he was a royalist, a cavalier if you like. He fought against Oliver Cromwell's army and went to France. He got shot in the leg and returned back here to Cornwall. "How did you find all of this out in just two days?" asked Dora. "We have the help of a company that does this for us from time to time," answered Susan. It seems that Abe came into money at sometime, for in 1684 he bought a sizeable piece of land on the coast. It was registered with the newly formed land registry of 1662. Then he had the headstone put on the unmarked grave in the churchyard again in 1684.

We have no proof, but we think that Frenchy on the stone refers to the man's origin rather than his name. What we don't know is where did he Abe, get the money to buy the land? And why did he pay for a headstone? Did he know this man from sometime in the past? If so, why didn't he have his proper name put on the stone? One thing we do know is that piece of land he bought has never been sold. It belongs to the only living member of the family, namely you, Tom!!"

"ME, really?"

"Yes, you Tom, as the only living Trevanion in this family line it's yours. Tom asked, "Do you know where this piece of land is, Susan?" "Yes, I have it marked on a map here." She took a printed piece of paper from her briefcase and handed it to Tom. "If you all would like to take a short walk with me I can show it to you."

They put on their shoes and followed Susan out of the cottage and down the road. When they came to Frenchy's cove and Rockfall point she swept her hand across them and said, "Tom, this is yours. Now why did he buy this piece of land, why not any other piece of land here-a-bout's?" They walked back to the cottage and Susan retrieved her briefcase and said to Tom, "The paper comes out tomorrow. Maybe it will jog someone's memory. She said goodnight, got into her car and drove off.

The next day the twins decided to have a day out in the boat with Tom and Ivan and leave the past in the past for a while. The three of them walked down to the harbour and climbed aboard Tom's boat. They set about getting everything ready for the off. Ivan was usually the first there in the morning. They were all looking out for him when they saw him and Alex walking towards them hand in hand. When they reached Eddie's boat Alex kissed him and boarded the boat. Ivan boarded Tom's boat with the local paper in his hand. "Hey, loves young dream I thought you said you and Alex were just old schoolmates. We have been waiting for half an hour for you to show your face," said Tom, with a twinkle in his eye and a broad grin on his face. "Well, you know how it is Tom, things move on."

"Well that's more than this boat is doing this morning," said Tom still with a smile. "Untie us and let's get out to sea."

Things were busy for a while, each of them doing what was expected of them and Tom heading the boat towards the distant crab and lobster pots. The twins fished for bait and Ivan baited the pots that were already onboard. When the boat slowed at the pots the real work began with Ivan hauling in the pots from the seabed and Benny and Manth measuring, sorting and securing claws. They were having a good day. The catch was above average and they then set off for the other pots further away. Ivan said, "I didn't know you were a landowner, Tom."

"What are you talking about, Ivan?"

"Take a look at the paper, Tom. And you two, it seems you are going to be rich if that story is right, and I've no reason to disbelieve it." Tom and the twins read the story in the paper. "Well?" said Ivan expectantly. "Is there any truth in it and if not where did they get those pictures of the coin and the golden cross from?"

When they were having lunch Tom told Ivan about his ancestry, about Abe Trevanion buying the land and paying for the headstone on Frenchy's grave in 1684. But he had no idea of why, or why he had never told anyone in the family that he owned it. "What about you two?" asked Ivan. Benny said, "A few days ago Manth and me found the items that are in the pictures in the paper. They are with the coroner at the moment and said to be worth a considerable amount of money. The coroner has to decide if it is treasure trove or not, but for what I have seen on the internet, as there is only two items and you wouldn't bury them in the sea intending to dig them up later it's probably not treasure trove. There doesn't seem to be any shipwrecks in the area, so it doesn't seem likely that it is that."

"So it will be yours then?" "Well, the land owner might have a claim." said Benny. "Where did you and Manth find it?" Asked Ivan. "Sorry we can't tell you that, Ivan."

"Well, Ivan, as we are telling all what's the story with you and Alex?" asked Manth "Not much really. We went to school together. She is a year older than me and we didn't really get on. I hadn't seen her for a couple of years, then I saw her on Eddie's boat. We got talking and went out a couple of times and now you might say we are an item." "Okay, said Tom, enough talking, let's see what we can catch." They each caught some fish for Dora to sell in the shop along with the crab and lobster. When they tied up at the quay side they stood talking to some other fishermen, who had all read the local paper and were interested in what land Tom had inherited. They also wanted to know where Benny and Manth had found the coin and cross. Benny said, "Sorry but we couldn't say where, because hoards of people would turn up with metal detectors and the landowner would not be happy about that." The fishermen all nodded in agreement.

Dora turned up in the van to take their catch and Eddie tied his boat up behind Tom's. "Hello, Squire," said Eddie, sweeping into a mock bow in front of Tom. "And how is my lord on this glorious afternoon?"

"I'll give you my lord, you old vagabond," said a beaming Tom, enjoying the good natured banter by his old friend. "I suppose you will be moving to some spacious manor house now, Dora!! And will his lord allow my lowly fish to be in the van with his more upper-crust catch? And these two soon-to-be millionaires, I suppose won't have the time of day for their old friends, Eddie and Alex." Benny replied, "I expect Manth and myself will spare a minute to pass the time of day with you humble fisher-folk." Having all had a good laugh they all went on their separate ways, Dora to the shop in the van, Tom and the twins to the cottage, Ivan and Alex hand in hand off to who knows where. Eddie stayed on his boat doing some jobs that needed his attention.

After dinner Susan turned up at the cottage. "Sorry to turn up without warning, but we might have a lead on going forward. A lady by the name of Layla Constantine phoned the office to say that in the early eighties while employed by the then-vicar of of Yarran's Shop she remembers having to take some books to the museum in Truro. She had a quick look at them at the time. One, she said, was written in foreign language, she thinks it was French, the others were diary's of a priest who was the vicar there in the 1680s. One of them mentioned a body on the beach, a book and a gold coin. The writing was in Old English and difficult to read, but she was sure the date was 1683."

"That's interesting," said Tom. "We are going to send Joe over in the morning to see if he can locate the books and have a look at them."

"I don't suppose he could take the twins with him, could he?" asked Tom. "I see no reason why not. I'll get him to stop by shall we say about nine o'clock in the morning," said Susan. "How did the paper's sales go today?"

"Fantastic, we are hoping it will be good all week, the story seems to have grabbed the people's imagination and if we uncover more, next week's sales might be even better. Right, I'll be on my way, sorry for the intrusion Tom."

Chapter VII

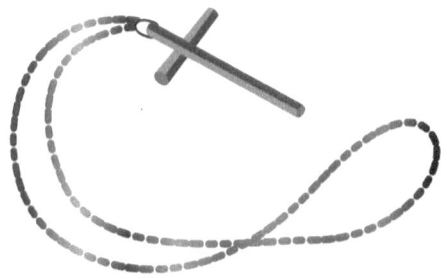

There was quite a bit of excitement at the breakfast table the following morning, for today the whole picture might become a lot clearer. Well, at least Manth and Benny were thinking that way. Tom told the twins that Truro was about 30 miles away and would take about 40 minutes in a car. Joe from the paper arrived a little after nine o' clock that morning. The twins said goodbye to Tom and Aunt Dora and climbed in the back of an ancient car with leather seats and the smell of age. Benny thought that perhaps Tom's estimate of 40 minutes might be a bit on the light side given the age of the car. Joe, like Dawn, was some sort of a Formula 1 racing driver, the old car roared like a lion when Joe found a straight piece of road.

They reached Truro in record time, a little shaken but not stirred, as Mr Bond would have said. After parking the car they walked to the museum and Joe found someone to help them after telling them who he was. Susan it seemed had phoned ahead and helped to make their mission a little easier. They were taken to a small room where a young man sat at a table with a little pile of books in front of him. "Hello I am Toby, Toby White," he said standing and shaking hands with each of them. "I understand you are interested in this collection of books. They have been sitting in the storeroom downstairs since I believe the 1980s, and had come from a church where they had been for some hundreds of years. Is there any particular one you are interested in?" Joe said, "We are given to understand that some of them are diaries of a priest who was the vicar of the church in Yarran's Shop."

"That is correct, any particular year?" asked Toby. "Have you one for the year 1683?" asked Joe.

Toby opened the diaries until he found one for 1683. "It must be your lucky day," he said. He handed Joe the book and a pair of white cotton gloves. "You won't mind wearing the gloves. will you, but these books are hundreds of years old?" Joe put on the gloves and turned the pages quickly until he came to September, then slowed down reading each page. After turning a few more pages his eyebrows shot upwards. "I think we have something here. It's about an old soldier with a wounded leg, finding a body on a beach after they had had a terrible storm for three days. The soldier had gone to the preacher telling him that he had found some stranger dead. He thought that he was French by his clothes. It says here that he had also found a book tied to his belt wrapped in waterproof sailcloth, and that the soldier had a small French gold coin that he wanted changing into silver. He said it was wrapped up with the book and was now his and if he tried to change it he would be cheated but no one would cheat a priest.

It says here that the preacher got the body collected, took his gold earring as payment for the interment, got the gold coin changed and took it to the hovel where the old soldier was living on The Beak. It also says that The Beak was different after the storm. The overhang that had given it it's name was gone and the cave that was underneath was gone. "Do you happen to have the book that the diary mentions?"

"The only book that isn't a diary is this one." He put a rather sorry looking specimen onto the top of the pile. "May I have a look?" asked Joe. "Be my guest, but it is not written in English," said Toby. Joe picked up the book and opened it. "It is written in French and not modern-day French." Joe was silent for a few minutes. This was written by a French corsair by the name of Jacques Devereaux in 1683."

"What was a corsair?" asked Manth. "If memory serves they were legalized pirates. The French government, for one, gave them a license to attack ships and ports and all booty was shared between the licensee and the government.

Jacques had a ship going by the name of Chien De Mer, or Sea Hound. He had on his ship two long cannon that were facing forwards. That was unusual and probably no ship no matter of what size had a defense against it. He could stand off and blast away out of range of most canon, at the same time presenting a small target, as he was facing head-on. Also he could attack from behind, where galleons and the like could not fire from. He was a clever man ahead of the game at that time. He tells of many places he had caused havoc, mainly in the Caribbean and ports on the Gulf of Mexico. He also attacked pirate ships. Then in 1683 he attacked a Spanish galleon called the Dinero Espiritu. My Spanish isn't very good but I think that might be Silver Spirit.

That galleon it turns out was on route from Veracruz in Mexico to Cadiz in Spain via Kingston, Jamaica and guess who lived in Jamaica in 1683!!" Joe read on in silence for a while turning pages. After what seemed like a long time to Benny and Manth, Joe started talking again. "When Jacques was attacking the galleon, which he did over a few days because his ship was much smaller and only using the two long guns so it took time to get the upper hand, the galleon's captain, whose name was Carlos Sanchez, went to see how his two passengers were."

"What two passengers?" asked Manth. "Oh, sorry, didn't I say, well, it seems Carlos was summoned by the King of Spain for a secret mission. Well, it seems Spain at the time was running out of money, but there was a lot of captured gold and silver held in Mexico. Carlos had to sail to Veracruz to secretly pick up the gold but also to bring a lady named Rosa Maria Dolores, who was one of the Spanish court's favorites and her maid, take them to Kingston to see her grandparents then return them to Spain.

To get back to the story, Carlos on getting to his cabin, which he had given to the two ladies, saw that the door had been smashed. Two of his crew had tried to take advantage of the ladies. Rosa stabbed one, killing him and the maid picked up his pistol and when the second man rushed in with his pistol at the ready the maid shot him. Carlos had them thrown overboard. After a few more days Carlos's galleon was boarded and sent to the bottom of the Atlantic, with only the two ladies and the captain kept for ransom. Captain Carlos revealed who the ladies were and all of the story up until Jacques had boarded his ship.

Then the weather took a hand in things. Jacques wrote down that they ran into sea fog, no wind and they didn't know where they were. They were drifting northeast and Jacques guessed that they were nearing the English Channel, with the hard granite shores of the southwestern English coast. After days the fog cleared and Jacques got his bearings. Then the weather changed again when a storm broke upon them like no storm that Jacques nor Carlos had ever seen. They had to take all the sail down but the wind was still driving them on, the skies were black by day and night, the rain lashed the deck and they were at the mercy of the terrifying waves. Jacques went out on deck and he could hear the waves crashing against rocks and see white foam in the near darkness. Walking back to his cabin he looked in his purse, seeing a few small French gold coins he filled his purse with gold coins from one of the chests. Those were the last lines he wrote in the log.

Joe closed the book, leaned back in the chair and looked at the twins. "So that is his story and that of the captain Carlos. We don't know what happened to the ship for sure, but somewhere along this coast a French corsair's ship lies wrecked. We thank you, Toby, for your time and patience. Now we are a lot closer to putting this puzzle together." Joe and the twins left the museum and went for a late lunch in a nearby cafe. "You can order whatever you like, the paper is paying," said Joe. Benny ordered a bacon baguette. "You will turn into a pig if you eat any more of their meat," said Manth, ordering a tuna and salad baguette. Joe ordered a sausage, bacon and egg bap. They found an empty table in a corner and keeping their voices low, they went over what they now knew.

Firstly we now know for sure that the grave in the churchyard is Jacques Devereaux's. We also know that Abe Trevanion paid to have the headstone put on the grave one year later. We also know that Rosa went to Jamaica and was on Jacques' ship and we are fairly sure the ship was wrecked locally because of the cross you found with Rosa's name on it and the date.

We also know that what we call Rockfall point was before the storm in 1683 called The Beak. Jacques' body was found on the beach of the cove now called Frenchy's cove, probably called that by good old Abe, after he bought it, because that's what he had put on the headstone. Also there is the French gold coin that Abe got the preacher to change that certainly came from Jacques. There is no mention of a purse on the body or a sword. Jacques had all of this gold and silver on his ship but no purse. Suddenly Abe, a beachcomber, buys land, pays for the headstone and has an inscription put on it that says thank you for the second chance in life. I think Jacques had a purse filled with gold coins and had a sword. A sea captain and pirate in those days never went anywhere without a sword.

I would put money on the fact Abe removed those things and hid them, taking only the small French coin and the book to the preacher. Telling him that, that was all the body had with him except for a gold earring to pay for his grave. After finishing their lunch they walked back to the old car and Joe drove them back to the cottage, where they both thanked Joe for a very informative day and he promised he would see them both soon, saying he would do some more digging. Tom came out of his workshop. "Have a good day in Truro?" he asked. "Yes, it was great and we have filled in a lot more holes in the puzzle. It will probably be better to go through it after dinner when Aunt Dora's here as well," said Benny.

With dinner finished and the dishes done and put away the twins related to Tom and Aunt Dora what they had found out at the museum. The first thing is we now know the name of the man buried in the churchyard. His name was Jacques Devereaux. He was a French corsair, that was a kind of pirate. He captured a Spanish galleon and he took the treasure that it was carrying and three people for ransom. The first was the captain of the galleon, whose name was Carlos Sanchez, his ship was called Dinero Espiritu. Joe thinks that means Silver Spirit. The second hostage was none other than Rosa Maria Dolores, the third was her maid. The French ship was named Chien de Mer, which Joe said means Sea Hound. They ran into sea fog that lasted for days and didn't know where they were, guessing that they were in or near the English channel. When the fog cleared they found their position, but the weather changed and they found themselves in a storm that neither of the captains had seen the like of in their lives. The ship was never seen again. We are pretty sure that Rockfall point was once called The Beak. It had a large overhang above a large cave but after the storm the overhang was gone and so was the cave.

Probably there was some kind of landslide of something. "When we were snorkelling that day I noticed some rocks on the seafloor that looked like they didn't belong there, they weren't bedrock." Joe thinks that Abe not only found the body of Jacques on the beach but also found his purse filled with gold coins and his sword. Abe relieved the body of those items and told the preacher there was only the book and a small French gold coin. Joe is going to do some more digging, but the logbook in the museum told us most of the story. Jacques kept records of all that happened from the day he had some special long cannons made and fitted to his ship, telling in detail how he fought the Spanish galleon, a much larger ship than his, using his long guns as he called them that fired directly forward. Carlos had no answer to that and after days of taking hits his ship was boarded and sunk.

The last things he wrote were about seeing the waves crashing against the rocks too late to do anything, so he filled his purse with gold coins, wrote his last words in the log, wrapped it in waterproof sailcloth, tied it to his belt and then was found drowned on the beach by Abe. Tom was amazed at what the twins had uncovered, things that had happened all of those years ago in a place he had lived in all of his life and knew nothing about. Benny and Manth had brought all of this to light in a couple of weeks of their holidays. "Where do you think the French ship sunk?" asked Aunt Dora. Benny said, "We found the coin and the cross on Rockfall point, which was, we think, once called The Beak. There was once a cave underneath it. Best guess is the ship was pushed up into the cave and a landslide occurred, sealing the cave entrance under tons and tons of rock.

Dora asked, "Do you really think that there is a remains of a French ship under what is now Tom's Rockfall point?" asked Aunt Dora. "We do, hence the names of the point and the cove," said Manth. "If that is the case, under those rocks is an absolute fortune just waiting to be discovered," said Tom. When the twins had left the kitchen table Tom asked Dora to bring her computer. "What do you want that for?" asked Dora. "I have heard of a thing called ground penetrating radar. It can tell what is beneath the surface. It might be silly, but maybe it could tell if there is indeed a cave or hollow beneath the rocks on the point." Tom spent some time surfing the net trying to find someone who could point him in the right direction. It took some time before he found someone with the equipment to do what he wanted. He noted down the phone number and put away the computer. "Find what you were looking for?" asked Dora. "I think so," replied Tom.

"Do you really think there is the remains of some foreign ship underneath Rockfall point?" Well let's look at the evidence, Dora. The coin and cross were found on the point. In 1683 there was a great storm that changed the appearance of the point, a French seaman was found washed up on the cove beach now called Frenchy's cove. Perhaps there was a cave under the point and perhaps there was a landslide that covered it up. Landslides are not uncommon, Dora."

"Have you found someone with the means to search?"

"I have the phone number of some guy. I'll phone him tomorrow and see what he has to say. It might not work on the point because of all of the rock and salt, but I'll find out tomorrow one way or another!"

"What if he tells you it stands a good chance of working, will you spend good money having it done?"

"Yes if only to fulfil the twins' investigations. They have worked hard on digging up the past, getting people interested and going back through my family tree, finding land that I didn't know I owned. They have both worked hard on the project. Yes, I'll pay for a search, Dora."

"You are just an old softy, Tom."

The next day the twins went to see Simon Drinkworthy, the vicar. First they tried the rectory, but he wasn't at home. They then went to the church, where they found Simon working on his sermon for the coming Sunday. "Hi, Simon, we have some news for you. Most of it will be in the local paper, but there was one thing we wanted to tell you before you read it in the paper. The person who is buried in the churchyard was a French corsair by the name of Jacques Devereaux and the book that was sent to the museum in Truro was his ship's log. It tells the whole story up until shortly before he drowned and was found by an old soldier on the beach, so you can update your burial records after over 300 years," said Manth.

"Thank you, both of you, for the work you have put into finding out who it was who was buried here all of those years ago."

"The man who paid for the headstone was a man by the name of Abe Trevanion, our uncle's great, great, at least ten times grandfather."

"Well, thanks again and by the way, who did you get to translate the book?"

"There is a chap who works for the paper by the name of Joe, who took us to the museum. He sat and read us some parts of it. He can read French and some Spanish," said Manth. "Ah, Joe, I know him. I've met him a couple of times in the past," said Simon.

The twins left the church and went back to the cottage, collected their swimwear, and went to the beach to enjoy the warm sunshine and just chill out. Tom meanwhile was phoning the number that he had found on the computer, the man's name was Charles Collins, the man whose number Tom had found on the computer. Charles answered the phone on the third ring. "Hello, Charlie here," he said. Tom said, "I found you while surfing the net and believe you do ground penetrating radar searches. Is that right?"

"Yes," replied Charlie. Tom told him what he needed and asked if the radar might do the job. Charlie's reply was that as long as the rock was not too thick it might well work, but the salt would not help. It appeared that Charlie had a free day the next day and could travel down from Plymouth and be there by mid-morning. Tom said he would meet him at the cottage the next day after giving Charles the address.

Tom told Ivan he might not need him in the morning unless he would go out with Benny and Manth, as he had to meet someone tomorrow. Ivan said that if the twins were willing to go out with him, then he would captain the boat for the day. Tom said he would phone him when he had spoken to the twins later that day. When Tom came home the twins were still at the beach so Tom spent some time in his workshop with his model galleon. He hadn't spent as much time here as he usually did, what with all that was going on with the find and the twins investigations into the past. When Manth and Benny came back from the cove, Tom asked them if they would go out on the boat with Ivan in the morning. "I have a chap coming to see me from Plymouth tomorrow morning, so I have asked Ivan if he would go out if you two would help. I have looked at the weather forecast for tomorrow and it is going to be like today, calm as a millpond." Benny and Manth both agreed to being the crew in the morning so Tom phoned Ivan and told him that the twins would be at the harbour in the morning.

Tom gave the twins a call in the morning, and Dora made them breakfast and when they left for the harbour Dora gave them a packed lunch and one for Ivan. They set off for the short walk to the boat, calling out to Eddie and Alex as they passed by his boat. Ivan was waiting for them, having got everything ready for the day. Morning to you both, let's make your uncle proud of us today by getting a good catch. Ivan took the boat out of the harbour, tooting the horn as they passed Eddie and Alex. Manth fetched two fishing rods and a bucket and she and Benny started catching bait for the pots. When they had some fish Benny started baiting the pots as Ivan had shown him on previous trips. Ivan looked back from the little cabin and gave them a thumbs up.

Charles Collins stopped his pickup truck outside the cottage and rang the doorbell. Tom answered the door. "You must be Charles," he said. "In the flesh, and you must be Tom," replied Charles. "Coffee," said Tom "or do you want to get on?"

"Coffee would be fine, it's quite a step from Plymouth to here." Charles followed Tom into the kitchen and sat at the table while Tom made the drinks. "What exactly are you looking for on this piece of land?" asked Charles. Tom not, wanting to give too much away, told Charles about the piece of land called The Beak in 1683 that had a cave underneath a large overhang. After a very violent and long-lasting storm the overhang and the cave had disappeared. The piece of land we are going to probe today is called Rockfall point. What we are trying to find out today is if the point has a cave beneath it and so The Beak and Rockfall point are one and the same place.

When they had finished their coffee they drove down to the point, where Charles walked to the end of the point then walked back to his pickup truck. "Right, Tom, I'll have a go." He took some equipment from his truck and set off walking sticking a probe into the ground every few feet, towards the end of the point. He walked up and down the point, moving over a couple of feet with each pass, until he had covered every foot of the ground. The time had passed into the afternoon before Charles put his equipment back in the pickup truck. Taking out his computer, he typed in a few instructions and a picture appeared. Pointing out some things, Charles said "Look here, Tom, and again here. I'm pretty certain that there is a void beneath this lump of rock, but I can't tell you the dimensions because the thickness varies and I can't penetrate it in places."

"Well, thank you for the work you have put in here today. Do you want another coffee as you worked through your lunch break?"

"No thanks, Tom, as I said earlier, it's quite a step from Plymouth to here, so I'll be pushing on home. I'll email you the computer printout and my invoice. I hope what I've found is what you are looking for. Cheers, bye."

Tom walked back to the cottage unsure of his next step. It would take some thinking about and some discussion with Dora and the twins. When Tom got home the twins were waiting for him. "Hi, Tom, when we were coming in there was someone walking about on the point with something like a walking frame."

"He was the reason I didn't go out in the boat today. He came over from Plymouth. His name is Charles Collins and he does ground penetrating radar. That was the thing you thought was a walking frame."

"What is ground penetrating radar when it is at home? asked Benny. "It sends a radar pulse into the ground that tells you what is beneath the surface. I will get the computer printout later on this evening."

"Can it tell if there is a shipwreck there?" asked Manth. "Probably not. What I'm hoping for is if there is a void underneath the point, If there is then we will be pretty sure that The Beak and Rockfall point are the same place.

That evening Tom got out the computer and looked at the emails, there was one from Charles. Tom opened the email along with the attachment and they all crowded around looking at the picture. With the help of the explanation at the bottom they could see what the GPR had seen that afternoon. After studying the picture Tom pointed out what looked like a void under the point. Right, we need to discuss the way forward. One, we can say if there is a French ship under the point, it can just stay there and forget about it. Two, we can get a contractor to open up the point. It will cost, but we can probably afford it. Three, if there is a cave and the remains of a ship with an untold fortune, then we will have to employ security 24/7 to keep treasure hunters out.

Benny and Manth talked to each other in hushed tones for a minute or two before Manth said, "Tom, Benny and me are willing to use whatever money we get for the coin and gold cross, although some of it belongs to you as you are the landowner." Dora said. "That's very generous of you both, but you don't have to do that. Tom and I can afford to get someone to make a hole so that we can explore further."

"Okay, said Tom, we all seem to be agreed to carry on with this project and see whether or not there is a boatload of treasure down there. I've been enjoying this little adventure, so let's go for it." Tom phoned one of his friends and asked if he could come over and see him about a job. The voice on the other end of the phone said he would be there in ten minutes.

Terry Broadbent true to his word turned up ten minutes later, "What can I do for you Tom, my old friend?" Tom said, "Take a stroll with me Tel, it's only a couple of hundred yards." Tom and Tel walked off towards the point chatting away and half an hour later they were leaning against Tel's Range Rover. They shook hands and Tel drove off. Tom came back into the kitchen with a broad grin on his face, made a cup of coffee and sat down at the table. "What did he say, Tom?" asked Dora. "Right, well, he will give it a go, but he isn't sure his equipment is up to the job. But then again, he has a friend who can do it. It's a little noisier but very quick."

"Sounds like he is the man to help out. How can he do it that much quicker?" asked Dora. "Because he is an explosive engineer. He will drill a few small holes, put in small charges and boom!! A big hole in the rock."

"Sounds very exciting," said Benny.

Tel arrived the next morning with his equipment and crew and they spent the day toiling away on the point while the twins sunbathed and swam in the cove. At about three o' clock. Tel took out his phone and phoned someone. A few minutes later Tom walked up onto the point and Tom and Tel talked for a few minutes before Tel took out his phone again. He phoned someone else and spoke to them for a few minutes. Then putting his phone away, he spoke to Tom again. Finally they all left, going their separate ways, Tom walking towards the cottage and Tel leaving in his Range Rover. Manth and Benny packed up their towels and things and walked over to the point and looked at the place where Tel and his crew had been working. Seeing they had not made much of an impression on the tough granite, the twins left the point and headed towards the cottage.

When they reached the cottage Tom was in his workshop, softly whistling to himself and working on his galleon. "Hello, Tom," said Manth. "Hi, Manth, and Benny. Had a good day down at the cove?"

"Yes, we saw you talking to Tel and we had a quick look at what Tel and his crew have done today. Not that impressive."

"No, it wasn't, but Tel has some help coming tomorrow. It will go faster then, I can guarantee. His long-time friend Boom Boom MacRae is coming over from the moor, Bodmin moor that is."

"That's a funny name," said Benny. "His real name is Jamie MacRrae, but everyone calls him Boom Boom because he's an explosive engineer. He will be here in the morning.

In the morning Tom had left for his boat, the twins were having breakfast and Tel was having coffee in the kitchen with Dora. A fluorescent green and orange truck pulled up at the cottage. Written across it in black letters was Have your problem Blown Away By Boom Boom MacRae. When the doorbell rang, Dora showed the man into the kitchen. "Morning, I'm Jamie, but everybody who knows me on the planet calls me Boom Boom, "Coffee." said Dora. "Seeing as my old friend Tel has a mug full, that would be nice, thanks. Black with one sugar, please."

"Does everyone really call you Boom Boom? asked Manth."

"Yes little lady, everybody does." When they had finished their coffee Tel and his crew left for the point followed by Boom Boom in a truck that you could quite easily see from the moon.

"Are you two going to the cove again today?" asked Aunt Dora. "Yes, we thought we might go snorkelling for a while."

"Well, stay away from the point. I don't want you anywhere near those explosions."

"Yes, Aunt Dora, we won't go anywhere near the point." said Benny, although Benny knew that he would be attracted to it like iron to a magnet. Dora set off to the shop in the van and Manth and Benny set off for Frenchy's cove in their wetsuits with their towels and snorkelling gear. As they passed the point they could plainly see the truck and the Range Rover parked at Rockfall point.

Manth and Benny laid out their towels on the sand. Although it was still before mid-morning the sun was becoming quite hot. There wasn't a cloud in the bright blue sky and the water looked cool and inviting. The twins walked down to the water's edge put on their masks, flippers and snorkels and walked backwards into the cool blue waters of the cove. They soon found the seahorses in the seagrass that they had seen on their previous visits to that part of the cove. They stayed watching them for a while before swimming away in search of other interesting sights. After about two hours of snorkelling they headed for the beach and stretched out on their towels and had their lunch.

While eating their lunch with their backs leaning against a warm smooth rock, they both cast their sight to the activity on Rockfall point. Boom Boom and Tel's crew were working drilling holes in the granite. Tel was unloading what looked like long lengths of wide, heavy rubber. By the time they had finished eating the drilling had stopped. Boom Boom was pushing what Benny imagined was explosives down the holes. An electric cable was laid from the drilling site to the vehicles, then the whole thing was covered with the heavy rubber strips. All of the men returned to the relative safety of their vehicles, climbing in and closing doors and windows, with the exception of Boom Boom MacRae, who was fixing the wire cable to some sort of box. He looked all around and sounded a loud horn attached to an aerosol can, There was a muffled boom and the rubber strips lifted for a brief moment then collapsed back to where they had been amid a small cloud of smoke and dust.

Boom Boom walked back to the drilling site, then

waved the rest of them back over and they dragged the rubber strips from where they had been placed. They all stood there for a few seconds looking down, then started doing high fives. "Looks like a success," said Benny. Boom Boom, Tel and his crew walked back to Boom Boom's truck and unloaded some red and white striped fencing and some warning signs. They then made a cordon around the explosion site, walked back to their vehicles, shook hands and drove off towards the cottage. "Well, that wasn't very exciting, was it Manth?"

"What were you expecting, a big bang, smoke and flames with pieces of granite falling out of the sky? This isn't the movies, Benny, this is serious stuff. There is health and safety these days, laws on what you can and what you can't do. It's not like the wild West, where they put a piece of fuse in a stick of dynamite, lit it threw it down a hole and just wandered off. People get killed working with explosives and we don't want that do we?"

"No, of course not Manth, I just thought it might be a bit more of a spectacle, that's all.

Later on in the afternoon Tom walked down to Benny and Manth carrying a big torch and a weight on a ball of twine. "Do you two want to have a look and see what is underneath Rockfall point? Tel phoned me and said they have a hole about three feet square." The twins packed up their things and followed Tom onto the point. Tom lowered the weight on the twine until it found the bottom, marked the place on the twine and pulled it up. He gave Benny the weight, then walked away until he came to the mark on the twine, then laying the twine on the ground he counted the paces back to Benny. "About twenty-five feet," he said. Then he turned on the big torch and shone it into the hole. There was nothing to see except damp sand and lumps of rock from the explosion. "Well, there is certainly a cave under Rockfall point and we are quite a way from the end of the point, so if there is anything in here it will be closer to the sea end than here."

Chapter VIII

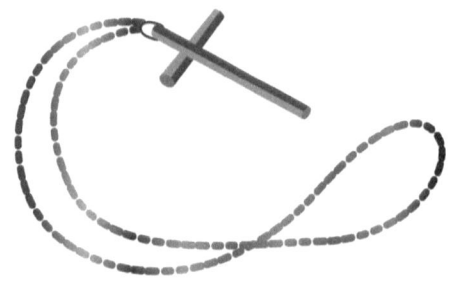

Tom searched around his workshop putting pieces outside to take to Rockfall point. He had some scaffolding squares that he used for painting the outside of the cottage. Also he had two pulley wheels, one with two wheels side by side, the other had a single wheel, a long rope, a harness he had borrowed from one of the lifeboat crew, a couple of hurricane lamps and three large torches. When Aunt Dora came home he borrowed the van and Tom, Benny and Manth loaded all of the things Tom had put outside of his workshop. They climbed aboard and drove off to the point. There Tom parked the van and they unloaded it, then carried the items up to the fencing around the hole. Tom put up the scaffolding squares that formed a square of six feet by six feet over the hole. He fastened two straight poles across the middle of the square, securing them with clamps. He then fixed the pulley with the two wheels to the middle of the two straight poles.

Taking the harness he fixed it to one end of the rope and threaded the other end of the rope through the pulley he had fixed to the cross poles. He then took a metal spike and hammered it into the ground close to the hole. Fixing the other pulley to the spike, he passed the free end of the rope through that pulley, then passed the end of the rope through the other wheel on the double pulley. Tom explained that doing it this way it would only take half the effort to pull himself from the bottom of the hole to the top. He pulled the harness over to him, putting it on and showing the twins how to secure themselves into it when their turn came. Looking at his watch he saw that it was dinnertime so they returned to the van and returned to the cottage.

After dinner and the dishes were done they returned to the point. Even Aunt Dora came, explaining that they would probably kill themselves without her input. Tom put the harness on and taking a torch, the hurricane lamps and a box of matches he put on a pair of leather gloves and lowered himself into the hole, letting the rope slip through his hand. When he reached the bottom he lit one of the lamps and shouted for Manth to pull the rope up. When the harness came into view she grabbed it and the leather gloves that Tom had attached. Manth climbed into the harness. "You go careful, my girl," said an apprehensive Aunt Dora. "Don't worry aunt, Tom showed us how to put on the harness and I watched what he did with the rope," she said disappearing down the hole. Manth shouted up to Benny, who pulled up the harness, put the harness and gloves on and followed Tom and Manth down the hole, saying bye to his aunt as he did so.

By the time Benny had reached the bottom both of the hurricane lamps had been lit and all three torches switched on, casting light into corners of the cave that hadn't seen light for over three hundred years. Tom and the twins walked slowly in the direction of the sea, picking their way in the torch light and stepping over rocks that had fallen from the roof and walls over the years. Tom's torch picked up a long piece of wood in it's beam and they all bent down and looked at it. This was not just some driftwood for it had been planed and finished at some time. They carried on walking, taking care in the gloom. This was not the place or time to have a careless accident. They soon found more wood that had been finished, evidence of a wreck. The sand underfoot was becoming more damp and Tom supposed the sea water came up this far at high tide. Tom looked at his watch and noted that high tide was some way off yet. Another few yards they came to the first of the bones lying half buried in the sand on the floor of the cave.

Tom knelt down and studied them. "Human I'm afraid," said Tom to the twins. "Not completely unexpected if there is a wreck in here." Proceeding onwards they came to more bones, but this time there was a piece of wood driven into the sand carved with the name Carlos Sanchez. Benny, not believing what he was seeing in the light of the torches, said. "That was the name of the Spanish captain who was taken prisoner when Jacques sank his galleon," Tom said. "Well that proves all that we have thought. Somewhere in this cave we are going to find more things but not tonight. It's time we were getting back. Dora will be worried. We also need a lot more light, and I have an idea where to find the very thing."

The three of them walked back towards the roof opening with the hurricane lamps and the harness. "Okay, Manth, you go first. Climb into the harness, put the gloves on, now put your arms above your head and catch hold of the rope you used to come down with. Now pull hand over hand and if you get tired before you reach the top squeeze both pieces of the rope together until your arms have rested." Manth pulled down on the rope with her right hand and her feet left the ground, then reached up with her left hand, pulled down and she rose further from the ground. "That's the idea, Manth, keep going." Manth soon reached the top, not needing to have a rest and Aunt Dora was there to give a hand getting her feet on terra firma. She put the gloves in the harness and sent it back down. "Okay, Benny, you next. Just do what Manth did and you'll be up in no time." Benny climbed into the harness, put on the gloves and shot off like a rocket.

Tom lifted the glass on the hurricane lamps and blew out the flame. The harness was already on it's way down. Tom switched off his torch and pulled himself to the surface. After getting out of the harness he pulled the rope all of the way through the pulleys, coiled it up and they all went back to the van. They all climbed into the van and Aunt Dora drove back to the cottage. Tom took out his phone and put in the number that he knew by heart. The phone rang three times, then a voice said, "Eddie here."

"Eddie, you old vagabond, have you still got the village's white L-E-D Christmas lights, the ones we put down the main road, in your lock-up?"

"Yes, why, Tom?"

"Any chance I can borrow them and your little generator for a few days, no questions asked?"

"As long as I get them back before Christmas," said Eddie. "I'll come over now, while I've got the van if it will be alright Eddie?"

"Yes, Tom, I'll go and open the doors. See you in five."

Tom drove the van over to Eddie's place. "I'm not going to ask any questions, Tom, just let me have them back in good order before it's time to string them up along the street at the beginning of December. If you need any help Tom, you only have to ask. I saw Jamie Boom Boom MacRae's truck leaving your place, so I guess it's got something to do with Rockfall point."

"Maybe, maybe not, Eddie." They loaded the lights and generator into Dora's van and Tom drove back to the cottage. On getting home he unloaded the borrowed items and locked them in the workshop. He went indoors and said. "Okay, we have lights and a generator. We will string them up tomorrow afternoon when I've finished work."

The twins went out on the boat with Tom and Ivan the next morning, All they really wanted to do was find whatever was in the cave under the point, but that had to wait until Tom was free to put up lights and get them working. The day seemed to drag by with every minute seeming like an age and they couldn't seem to be able to get interested in the day's work. "What's the matter with you two today? you don't seem to be yourselves?" asked

Ivan. "We have a lot to think about," answered Benny. Eventually it was time to return to the harbour, which seemed to brighten the twins' moods. They moored up in their usual place and Eddie followed, mooring behind them. Tom phoned Dora, telling her that they were in the harbour and could she send the van. Dora said, "Dawn would be there dreckly."

Dawn arrived in her usual fashion like some out of-work-racing driver "Hi, everyone," she said cheerily. Tom and Eddie loaded their catch into the van and Dawn sped off. Eddie said to Tom "Offer's still there, Tom." Tom said, "I'll think on it and let you know, Eddie." They all went their separate ways, Ivan hand in hand with Alex, the twins and Tom walking to the cottage, Eddie looking perplexed leaning against his boat. Tom unlocked his workshop and put the small generator on a sack truck, piled the lights around his and Benny's shoulders and gave Manth the rope and harness plus a bag of steel nails and a hammer. They walked down to the point, the twins now having a spring in their step.

Tom put the rope around the pulley wheels in the same fashion as he had done yesterday and he connected the lights to the generator and started it up. The L-E-D lights came on as bright as day. Helping Benny into the harness and giving him the gloves, he piled all of the lights around his shoulders and on his lap. Benny descended into the hole now lit up like a Christmas tree. On reaching the bottom he pulled the harness up to the top. Manth came down next with the hammer and nails and pulled the harness up for Tom.

Tom switched on one of the torches that they had left at the bottom the night before. Shining a light on the wall of the cave, he took a nail and hammered it into the rock.

They fixed the first L-E-D to the nail. Then all three walked along a few paces and hammered another nail into the rock and fixed the second light to it. They did this every few paces, leaving the cave lit up like it had street lights. They kept on hanging up the lights until they came to the place they had got to the night before. Tom moved on down the cave shining his torch ahead of him. Benny still had loads of lights in his arms so they could carry on towards the sea. Tom walked back and began hammering more nails into the rock and fixing the lights to them. He shone the torch into the darkness in front of them, when blocking the way was a huge pile of wood. Benny walked forward climbing onto the pile.

"It's a ship!! Well, what's left of it." Benny hung lights everywhere he could hang them and soon the pile of wood was lit up so that they could see it clearly. "This is the Sea Hound, isn't it Tom?" said Manth. "I don't think there is any doubt about that. This thing is going to be too big for us. We are going to need help. Which means we will have to share around whatever is in here. Now it's up to you two, you were the two who started this hunt." Benny said, "That's alright with me." Manth agreed. Who do you suggest help us, Tom?" asked Manth. "Eddie has already asked, and perhaps Ivan and Alex, people we know and trust."

"That sounds like a good idea to me," said Benny.

Tom walked up to the hole in the point, took out his phone, looked to see if he had a signal and dialled a number from memory. After two rings it was answered. "Hi, you old reprobate, are you busy? If not, get your body over to the point, pronto. I need your help."

"I'm on my way, Tom," said Eddie. Tom climbed into the harness and pulled himself to the surface. Eddie drove up in a cloud of dust a few minutes later.

"What's the problem Tom?"

"First, I need to swear you to complete secrecy, Eddie old mate."

"That goes without saying, Tom, you know that." Tom said, "Right lower yourself down this hole." Eddie climbed into the harness and lowered himself down like he did so ever day of his life. Tom followed Eddie. Once on the bottom he said, "Follow the lights but be careful of the bones. They have been down here for over three hundred years." Eddie and Tom walked down the cave until they came to the broken and rotting ship. "What have you got here, Tom?" "Well, you remember the twins finding those things a few days back? Well, they came from this. It's the remains of a French corsair's ship called in English, Sea Hound. We believe it is carrying a fortune in gold and silver from 1683."

"Don't you have to report it to the authorities?"

"Yes if it comes under buried treasure we have to do it in seven days, but we haven't found anything yet. If it's a wreck we have to report it within fourteen days. We don't know what it is, so we need to find whatever is in there quickly. I'm going to phone Ivan and Alex to see if they might be interested."

While Tom and Eddie were talking, Benny climbed out from under some of the timbers and showed Manth what he had in his clenched fist. Manth's eyes nearly popped out of her head. Benny said to Eddie, "Do you want to help?" Eddie said, "There might not be anything in here worth having." Benny replied, "That might be so, but when you've just found these." Opening his hand and putting the contents of his hand into Eddie's he said, "of course there just might be." Eddie stared down at the three coins that Benny had just put in his hand, two of silver and one gold. Eddie gasped and said, Boy, they are worth more than I earn in a month. Might be more then I earn in a year. Is there any more?" "Are you in or out, Eddie?" asked Tom.

In way of an answer Eddie said, "Let's move some of this loose timber against the cave wall so that we can see what's what." Tom looked at his watch. They would only have about an hour before dinner and Tom wasn't going to upset Dora by being late, not for all of the hidden treasure in this cave. They all worked hard for the next half an hour stacking the loose timber against the wall. Manth saw something glimmering on the sandy floor. She bent down and scraping about in the sand picked up another three coins. "Okay, let's go to dinner," said Tom. Are you going home or eating with us, Eddie?"

"If there is enough I'll eat with you and Dora. My good lady is out tonight I was going to nuke a dinner for one."

"What do you mean nuke a dinner for one?" asked a somewhat bewildered Manth. "What he means is, he was going to put a frozen dinner for one in the microwave," said Tom with a grin. "Yeh, nuke it," said Eddie.

Tom walked into the kitchen and said to Dora, "Can you stretch dinner for one more?"

"Not a problem, Tom, why, who is coming?"

"This old reprobate," he said as Eddie walked in. Dora agreed, "Seeing as it's you, Eddie, it will be a pleasure," and Tom announced to her, "Eddie has become the newest member of our little treasure hunter's club."

"Look Aunt Dora," said Manth putting the six coins on the kitchen table. Dora asked, "Where did you find these?"

"We have found the ship under Rockfall point. If Jacques' log is right there could be thousands of these down there."

"We need help, so Eddie is helping. We going to ask Ivan and Alex as well. Keep it between friends," Tom said.

After dinner and the clearing up done they headed back to the point. Dora said "I'm coming too."

"Are you sure you want to do this, Dora?" asked Tom. "If you, Eddie and the twins can do it, then so can I," said Dora. They were soon all in the cave, making their way to the remains of the ship. "I recognise these lights. They're the village Christmas lights, aren't they Tom?" asked Dora.

"Yes, we sort of borrowed them for a while," said Tom. They walked to where they had started stacking the timbers before dinner. Tom said, "Right, let's shift this loose timber away and see what we have here. All five of them toiled away, stacking the timbers against the cave wall. After about an hour most of the loose timber had been moved and Benny climbed into what would have been the hull of the ship. All of what would have been the deck and cabins had collapsed to its lowest point.

Benny edged his way in further. Tom said "Be careful in there, my boy, I'm not sure how stable it is."

"Okay, Tom, but I think I can see something. It's a bit dark but, yes, there is something here." A few minutes later Benny emerged from the hole he had climbed into, holding out his hands to Manth, who was closest. "Here, grab this, Manth, I'm going back in. There is more where that came from." He disappeared back into the hole, where Manth could hear him crawling about in the semi-darkness. She passed the items that Benny had given her to Eddie and climbed into the hole after Benny. Crawling up to where Benny was, her eyes adjusting to the dim light, she could see lots of glimmering objects. She picked up gold and silver coins and small pieces of ancient jewellery, putting what she could into her pockets to make room in her hands for picking up more.

Manth, then Benny climbed out of the hole, giving Tom, Eddie and Aunt Dora the things they had retrieved from the wreckage. "Do you know what you have here?" asked Eddie. "These things are either Aztec, Inca or Mayan. They are worth an absolute fortune today."

"Some of these things are beautiful," said aunt Dora. "What are we going to do with this stuff? I don't want it in the house, and we will have to secure the entrance to this cave. If one word of this gets out we will have every treasure hunter and criminal in the country making their way here," said Tom. It was agreed that Tom would get Tel to fit some sort of trapdoor. with some urgency, bolted into the rock with some heavy duty locks, "I'll tell him it's dangerous to leave it open, in case someone falls in. We will have to dismantle the scaffolding until Tel has done the work and those things I will hide where they can't be found for the time being.

They dismantled the scaffolding and put it in Eddie's jeep along with his generator, the rope and pulleys. They went back to the cottage and unloaded everything into Tom's workshop and took the treasure into the kitchen to look at it in the better light. After everyone had looked at it and photographed it Tom fetched a tin box from the workshop and they placed all of the items into it and closed the lid. Eddie said, "What are you going to do with it?" Tom said, "Better nobody knows, but it will be safe." Tom lifted a garden slab, dug a hole and placed the tin inside, then replaced the slab standing on it to settle it.

Tom phoned Tel, and after a few minutes of

conversation Tom walked back into the kitchen saying "Okay, the treasure is hidden and Tel is sending a couple of his crew tomorrow. He is busy so he can't come himself. I have told him what I want and he said they could manufacture it themselves on site and fix it securely. I'll phone Ivan and see if he wants to join us. If you, Eddie would ask Alex, tell her there might be enough in it for her to buy a decent motorbike." Eddie took out his phone and called Alex. After a couple of minutes he put his thumb up. "Alex is in," he said. Tom phoned Ivan. The phone rang once and Ivan's voice said, "Yes," then rang off. Alex had obviously spoken to Ivan when Eddie had phoned her.

Tel's crew arrived at Rockfall point the next morning with two sheets of heavy duty steel, grinders, a welder and a rock drill. They set about making a trapdoor and securing it to the rocks with long bolts screwed into the granite. When the doors were closed they covered the bolts so that they could not be unscrewed. They fitted two large padlocks and locked it, taking the keys to the cottage and telling Tom who had just got in, that the job was finished. "Nobody is going to get down there anytime soon without those keys," said one of the crew. Tom took a stroll down to Rockfall point, walking to the place where the hole was. There was a new trapdoor. Tom took the keys from his pocket, unlocked the new padlocks and lifted the door. He examined the bolts that were screwed into the rock. He closed the door again, noting that the bolts were covered by the door so that they could not be unscrewed with the door closed and locked. Tom locked the padlocks and with a satisfied smile walked back to the cottage.

Tom walked into the kitchen. Opening a drawer he placed the padlock keys in a small metal box. Closing the drawer he said to the twins, "They have done a good job. Nobody is going down into the cave without those keys. Everything down there is safe now." One hour later Tom received a phone call from a woman whose name was Cassie Luxton. She was the finds liaison officer for Cornwall. "Can I come and see you tomorrow?" she asked. "It is to do with the coin and pendant that a Benny and Samantha Franks found at a place called Rockfall point."

"Is there a problem?" asked Tom. "Only in as much as that you took the finds to the coroner and they should have come to me. I would like to see the exact spot that they were found."

"I shall be at my cottage by about two-thirty tomorrow afternoon. I will have the twins here with me. as they are the only ones that know where exactly the items were found. Do you have the address of the cottage?"

"Yes, so until tomorrow I will bid you goodbye. Tom told the twins about the phone call and what this Cassie Luxton wanted. The next afternoon Tom, Eddie and the twins loaded Eddie's jeep with all of the things they would need to go down into the cave and waited for Cassie Luxton.

Ten minutes later an old Land Rover pulled up at the cottage and a trim red- haired young lady climbed out of her vehicle. "Hello, I am Cassie Luxton, which one of you is Tom?" Tom walked over to her and said, "I'm

Tom, this is Eddie and those two are Manth and Benny." Right, shall we take a short walk to where the two items were found? The twins they are the only ones who know exactly where it was." While Manth, Benny, Tom and Cassie walked to Rockfall point Eddie drove his loaded jeep to the new cave entrance. Manth and Benny showed Cassie where they found the coin and the pendant explaining how the coin had attracted Benny's attention and how he had made a tool to retrieve them the next day. Cassie took photos and spoke into her phone, making a short video.

"Thank you both, I can now make my report," said Cassie. "Before you go, perhaps you would walk over there to where Eddie is putting up that scaffolding square. We have something to show you that is connected to the twin's find. We only discovered this a couple of days ago after blowing a hole through the rock," said Tom. Eddie had erected the scaffolding and had attached the pulleys and after putting the rope through the pulleys and fixing the harness he descended down the hole into the darkness of the cave, returning a minute or two later with the light cable. "What is down there?" asked Cassie. "Oh, just some three-hundred-plus-year old French ship, complete with its stolen cargo of gold, silver and artefacts taken from a Spanish galleon," said Tom. "You are teasing me, right?" said Cassie. By this time Eddie had connected the light cable to the generator and started it up. The twins and Eddie descended into the hole. Then Tom showed Cassie how to get into the harness and how to slowly let the rope slip through her now gloved hands. When Cassie was safely down, the harness and gloves were pulled back up for Tom's descent.

Tom led the way down the cave, telling Cassie to be careful not to tread on the bones. "Bones!!" said Cassie. "This ship was pushed into this cave in a mighty storm sometime in 1683 and a landslide sealed the cave entrance behind thousands of tons of rock. So of course no escape was possible, all that were aboard that ship died in this cave. So yes there are bones."

"How could you possibly know," asked Cassie," "if it all happened in 1683?" Tom answered, "You have Benny and Manth, plus the local priest, the newspaper in Penzance, the museum in Truro and lastly, a French corsair who kept a ship's log."

They walked on down the cave towards the sea following the lights. When they came to the bones of Carlos Sanchez, with his name carved into the piece of wood, Cassie took out her phone and made another short video. They carried on walking until they came to the remains of the ship. "This is unbelievable, it's, it's… fantastic. How could a ship of this size possible get into this cave?"

"My guess is that the water was much deeper here three hundred years ago. I think the ship was pushed into the cave by large breakers, smashing off its masts as it was forced in, then when the landslide happened a large wave was created, pushing the ship further into the cave. Depositing a lot of debris on the cave floor, as the water receded the ship drifted back to the position that it is in now. As time has passed it has taken its toll on it, leaving what you now see." Benny clambered into the wreck, returning with a few coins and giving them to Cassie. She gasped at the sight of the coins in her hand and Benny said, "There are hundreds of them, maybe thousands."

Cassie took her phone out and placing the coins on the cave floor made another short video. "Okay, first we must inform the police. All human remains must be reported to them. They will send in someone to estimate their age, although we are pretty sure we can date them exactly. Then I will inform the ROW, that is the receiver of wrecks. They will send someone to see if it is classed as a wreck, or whether my department will take charge of It. I think it depends on the high water mark, but first I will phone the police." They all left the cave, with Tom instructing Cassie on how to pull herself to the surface. When Cassie was above ground she phoned the police, telling them about the cave and the human remains, saying that they may well be over three hundred years old. The person on the other end of the phone said they would send the appropriate people as soon as possible, asking for the exact location.

Cassie then spent some time on the phone to her superior, asking for advice, and then spoke to the ROW people. They said they would send someone over as soon as was possible, asking for her phone number. Eddie drove down to the village and returned with coffee for them all. They all sat in Eddie's jeep drinking their coffee, when a chap from the police forensics department arrived. He introduced himself and Tom and Cassie took him down into the cave, showing him the bones. After taking photographs from every possible angle he told Tom and Cassie he would have to call and have them removed. When they came back out of the cave, Tom explained that there was a wrecked ship in the cave. So there are going to be a lot more human bones somewhere in the cave that they had not discovered as yet.

Cassie's phone rang. She answered and it was her superior, saying that he was on his way and hoped to be there in an hour. He asked Cassie if she would mind staying until he arrived so she could brief him on the situation. Cassie agreed to his wish and said she would see him soon. She was just going to put her phone in her pocket when it started ringing again. It was from someone at the ROW saying they would have someone over tomorrow if that would be okay. "Can you hold on for a minute, as I will have to clear it with the landowner?" Cassie asked Tom if the ROW people could come over tomorrow. "Yes," replied Tom, "there would be someone here."

"That will be okay," said Cassie into her phone.

Within an hour Cassie's superior arrived. He climbed out of his car and exchanged a few words with Cassie, then introduced himself to Tom. "My name is Peter George. I understand that you are Tom Trevanion. Can I see the finds?" he asked. Tom took him to the cave entrance and helped him into the harness and giving him the gloves he showed him how to lower himself. Turning to Eddie he said "The lights if you would, please." Eddie started the generator. "I will follow you down. Send up the gloves and harness," said Cassie. When the gloves and harness were back at the top

Cassie lowered herself back down into the cave. Tom, Eddie and the twins sat around talking, waiting for Peter and Cassie's return. After about three quarters of an hour Eddie said, "I hope they are alright down there." It was another twenty minutes before Peter's head appeared above ground. Tom helped him out of the harness and sent it and the gloves back down for Cassie. Cassie joined Peter and the rest of them. "Quite a find you have here, Tom. I'm hoping that we can do the excavations. This is most exciting, but the ROW might claim it as theirs. I understand that they will be here tomorrow. If you don't mind I would like to come back with Cassie tomorrow, would that be possible, Tom?"

"I see no reason why not," answered Tom.

As they were leaving the people turned up to retrieve the bones. "Busy here, isn't it," said Eddie. "I'm afraid it's going to be like that for a while," said Tom. "I hope we don't get left out. After all, with all said and done it's our find and on my land as it turns out."

"Yes, as the newest member of the crew I'm looking forward to finding whatever secrets this cave has hidden for the last three hundred and more years," said Eddie. It wasn't long before one of the men appeared from the cave opening, followed by a wooden box and then the other chap. They thanked Tom, loaded the box into their van and left Rockfall point.

Eddie stopped the generator, then walked over to his jeep, bringing back some lengths of rope. First he secured a rope to the generator, then lowered it into the hole. Next he did the same to the two pulleys and then lowered them into the hole. Taking a piece of wire, he joined the two ropes leaving a loop, which he put over the place where the padlock would be put through, closed the door and secured the door with the two padlocks. Next he dismantled the scaffolding squares and taking another small padlock and a short chain from his jeep, he locked them all together, laying them on top of the cave door. Eddie climbed into his jeep and saying goodbye drove off home. Tom, Benny and Manth walked the short distance to the cottage. Tom said, "I have to work tomorrow, can the two of you open the trapdoor, put up the scaffolding and rig the pulleys ready for the people who are coming? I'm sure one of them will help you pull up the generator if you can't manage yourselves. Don't let them take anything away. If they try, run to the cottage and phone me, okay?"

Chapter IX

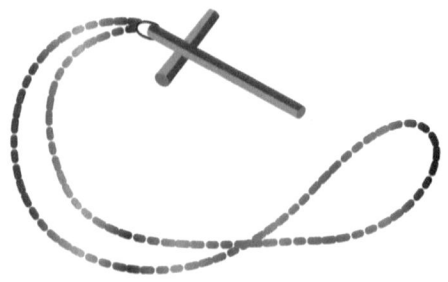

The next morning after having their breakfast, sausage, bacon and egg for Benny, a slice of toast and a yogurt for Manth, they took the padlock keys and walked off to Rockfall point. Unlocking the scaffolding they erected it over the trapdoor, then unlocking the padlocks they opened the door and pulled up the pulleys. Fixing the pulleys in place Benny pulled up the generator, which wasn't as heavy as he thought it would be. Everything now being ready they sat and waited and it was another hour before Peter and Cassie pulled up in Peter's car. They said good morning to the twins, then waited for the people from the ROW. A Land Rover rolled to a halt beside Peter's car and two people climbed out. "Morning all, who's in charge?" one of them asked. "That would be us. I'm Manth and this is my brother Benny. We were the ones that discovered the ship. This is Peter and Cassie from finds liaison office. Hi I'm Steve and this is Eve, we are from ROW, that is receiver of wrecks. Right, where are we going?" Asked Steve. "Down that hole," Benny replied. Steve next asked, "Do we need any light?"

"No, it's all taken care of. Follow me and Manth and I will get you safely down to the basement." They all headed to the scaffolding. Benny showed Steve and Eve how to put on the harness and how to descend slowly using the gloves and the rope. Eve went down first, then sent up the gloves. Steve went next, Followed by Cassie, Peter, Manth and lastly, Benny.

"Nice lighting system. It's almost like street lighting," said Steve. Manth led them down the cave to where the three hundred-plus-year-old ship lay in her final resting place. Eve bent down and looked at the coins that Cassie had laid on the sand and photographed the day before. "Is it alright to pick them up?" asked Eve. "Do you know what these are?" asked Steve. "We have a fair idea. There are gold and silver coins, mostly Spanish and Portuguese. There are artefacts from Central and South America, and somewhere, some cannon, from France that we haven't had time to find."

"How do you know all of that? Have you been doing your homework on line?"

"No, but we could tell you who the captain was and what ship he took this treasure from. Also the name of both ships and when this ship found her way into this cave."

"You know who was the captain of this ship?" asked Peter. "Yes," said a triumphant Benny. "I can show you his grave if you wish."

Eve asked, "Does the sea water come in here at high tide?"

"Not that we have seen since we have been coming

in here over the last few days," replied Manth. "You two seem to know a lot about this cave and what it contains. Would you like to enlighten us?" asked Steve. Manth related what they had found out, starting from the grave in the churchyard, then about the piece of paper that Simon Drinkworthy, the vicar, had found, naming the man who had paid for the headstone, which, with the help of the local newspaper and the museum in Truro, they had unearthed the French captain's log. Then the newspaper had traced Tom's ancestry back more than three hundred years and found out that Rockfall point and Frenchy's cove now belonged to him. With some detective work, some ground penetrating radar and some explosive, the cave, along with the ship, had been located.

"Quite a story and discovery by two children from Norfolk on a summer holiday with their uncle and aunt," said Cassie. "And now that the cave is secure, we will inform Susan at the newspaper, so that they can take some pictures and write the story in full as a thank-you for all of their help. At lunchtime Pete, Cassie, Steve and Eve all went to the village for lunch. Benny asked Manth if she would go to the cottage and bring him some lunch and at the same time phone Susan at the newspaper. Ask her if she could send someone with a camera to come to Rockfall point and look at their discovery this afternoon. "Can't you do it Benny?" asked Manth. "Yes, but you will have to look after the cave whilst I'm away, okay? Don't let anyone take anything. I'll be back as soon as I can, Manth."

Benny ran to the cottage and phoned Susan at the

newspaper, making himself a peanut butter and Marmite sandwich and a tuna salad sandwich for Manth. He looked in the fridge and found two cans of fizzy drinks, put it all in a sandwich box and headed back to Rockfall point. When he got back Manth was sat on the generator, idly throwing small pebbles, trying to hit a small rock a short distance away. "What did you get me for lunch?" she asked. "Same as me, peanut butter and Marmite sandwich."

"Oh, no, that's disgusting. I'm not eating that."

"All the more for me," said Benny, opening the sandwich box. "Give me a small bite, then," relented Manth. She closed her eyes and took a small bite of the sandwich that Benny put in her hand. "That's, that's horrendous, how could you ever eat that?!!" Manth wailed.

"Well, you had better have this one Manth, it's tuna and rabbit food," said Benny. "Why, oh why, did I have to have a brother?"

"Because brothers are better," said Benny.

An hour later a small procession of cars arrived at Rockfall point. First was Peter and Cassie, next was Steve and Eve and then Joe in his ancient road rocket. Steve said, "We have discussed this over lunch and talked to the powers that be and we all agree that this would be best investigated by Pete and Cassie's team from the museum. So we will bid you farewell and wish you the best of luck." With that Steve and Eve climbed back into the Land Rover and drove off. "Who is this?" asked Cassie. "Sorry Cassie, this is Joe from the local newspaper. He has been helping us with our detective work. Joe, this is Pete and Cassie from the museum. Shall we descend to the basement?" said Manth. Benny started the generator, while Manth supervised the descent into the cave.

"How did you locate this cave?" asked Joe. "With a lot of help, from a lot of kind people," said Manth. "If the treasure that was in the captain's log is still on the ship it will put Yarran's Shop well and truly on the map," said Joe. When Joe had taken all of his photos of the remains of the ship and the treasure that was at the moment visible on the floor of the cave, he took some pictures of the twins. Then he asked Peter and Cassie if he could take their pictures as well. They both agreed, so he snapped away. Then they all went back above ground just as Tom and Eddie arrived. Tom introduced himself and Eddie, telling them all that he was the owner of Rockfall point. Joe then took their pictures. Cassie then said to Benny, "When Steve asked how you knew all of the history of the ship and cave, you told him that you knew the name of the captain of the ship. You also said you could show him his grave. Could you show it to me?"

"Yes, of course, if you don't mind a walk to the churchyard," answered Benny. "I would like a picture of that. We could ride up in my car, as I am going that way," said Joe.

Cassie, Manth, Benny and Joe climbed into the car and drove the short distance to the church. Benny took them to the now clean gravestone with its now readable inscription. "This is it," said Benny. Joe took some pictures. "I thought you said you knew his name. It just says Frenchy on here," said Cassie. "When Uncle Tom's ancestor paid for the headstone, he didn't know him or his name, but he was dressed like a Frenchman. So Frenchy is what he had the mason put on the stone."

"So, what was his name? Asked Cassie. "I can answer that," said Joe. "When the twins and I went to the museum in Truro, I read the captain's log. It was written in French and his name was Jacques Devereaux. The captain of the ship he stole the treasure from was a man named Carlos Sanchez. Cassie had recorded all of this on her phone, saying all this would help her and Peter in the future. Joe bade them all a good afternoon and walked to his car and drove off, the twins and Cassie walked back to Rockfall point.

That evening Susan from the paper phoned Tom. Would it be convenient to come to the cottage after dinner for a talk? Tom said they weren't doing anything special so by all means come. Susan arrived after they had had dinner and cleaned the dishes away. "I hope you don't mind me coming at this time of the day, but I don't seem to get a minute to myself during the day and there are a few things I need to go over with you all."

"No, this suits us all," said Tom. I have seen the photos that Joe has taken from the cave on Rockfall point, I am no expert, but I think in today's market this is going to be worth a considerable fortune."

"That is what we are led to believe," answered Tom. Susan went on, "I just need to confirm a few things. Joe is writing up most of it, as he has been to see the wreck and he has read the captain's log. After she had asked all of her questions she said, "We are putting this as the lead story on the front page. It will go National, so you will have reporters and possibly television crews on your doorstep. It's going to put your little village on the map, all of you will be in the public eye until the next big thing comes along."

After Susan had left, Tom asked if the twins and Dora were ready for what would almost certainly happen in the next few days. "I shall be alright for most of the day, being out on the boat. I don't suppose that any reporters will follow us out to sea. But you, Dora, you will be in the shop all day and they are bound sure to want to talk to you. Manth, you and Benny will have to be at the cave to help Peter and Cassie and their team get in and out of the cave. That means there will be lots of the press and maybe the television people trying to get pictures. So you two will be in the limelight for most of the time, are you alright with that?"

"Yes," said Benny. "And you, Manth?" asked Tom. Manth answered, "If you had asked me that question before we started this holiday, I would have probably said no. Now after all of the detective work we have all put into it, I shall play the superstar, so yes I'm up for it, Uncle Tom."

"I will bring Eddie, Ivan and Alex when we have finished on the boats tomorrow, so that Pete and Cassie can meet the whole team. I don't want anyone left out. I will ask Peter or Cassie to call into the shop to meet Dora, as it's difficult for her to come to the cave."

The next afternoon the cave seemed to be full of people, what with the team that worked with Peter and the crews from Tom's and Eddie's boats, plus the twins. Peter organised everyone so that they each had a job to do and it seemed to work without any problems. Peter explained that it would take weeks of work to uncover everything that the cave had kept hidden for the last three hundred-plus years. Everything had to be photographed, logged and removed systematically, not just the treasure, but the day to day things that the crew used like tools, knives, cups, plates, oil lamps, anything that hadn't rotted or rusted away, any items that would shed a light on the life aboard a ship from the seventeenth century.

It was two days later when the press and the television crews descended on the little Cornish village. Dora was doing a roaring trade, selling her wares to the strangers, who all wanted to know where this French treasure ship that had been found locally was. Dora told them all about the twins and the detective work that had eventually led to the uncovering of the ship from its hiding place in the cave under Rockfall point. She also told them about the grave of Jacques Devereaux in the churchyard, saying that it was the discovery, of his unmarked grave and the finding of the cross and coin that inspired the twins to investigate the link between Frenchy's cove and Frenchy on the later-added headstone on the grave. "Where is this Rockfall point?" asked one of the reporters. "Oh, just follow the road on past the harbour and up the rise. On your right will be a big piece of land sticking out into the sea. That's Rockfall point." All of the strangers left the shop eating their pies and pasties, jumped in their vehicles and disappeared in the direction of Rockfall point.

The first of the television crews stopped at Rockfall point just as the first of the long cannons was being lifted out of the cave into the bright summer sunlight. Peter had installed a stronger lifting platform for just this event. "Jeff, Jeff are you getting this?" said a television presenter to a cameraman. "Got it, Martin," replied the cameraman. "Okay, guys, get over there and keep that camera rolling, don't stop until I tell you."

"You're the boss, Mar," said Jeff. "Don't call me that, you make me sound like an old woman."

"Precisely," answered Jeff. Within a couple of minutes there were news crews everywhere, trying to get interviews with anyone who looked like they were important. There, of course, was no one from the local newspaper, as Susan had already published the story along with pictures before she had informed the national press.

Peter had appeared above ground along with the cannon, somewhat taken aback by all of the media circus crowding around the cave entrance. "May I be of assistance?" he asked one of the television presenters. "We would like to speak to someone about the ship that is said to be in a cave here."

"Okay, I will send up my associate and the two people who know more about it than anyone else," said Peter. A few minutes later Cassie, Manth and Benny made an appearance from the cave. "Hello, I'm Cassie Luxton and this is Samantha and Benny Franks, but please call Samantha, Manth. The twins know more about this ship than anyone else after finding two items, a coin and a pendant. They gathered evidence piece by piece and with the help of their Aunt Dora and Uncle Tom they located the wreck in the cave under this piece of land. The ship, or what is left of it, is a French ship that was captained by a man by the name of Jacques Devereaux. Devereaux, we believe, was a corsair and he attacked a Spanish galleon, sinking it and taking the vast treasure that it was carrying back to Spain. Caught in a three day storm, it ran aground and was pushed into the cave."

"As that happened there was a massive landslide that covered the entrance with thousands of tons of rocks and debris. This caused a massive wave that pushed the ship further into the cave and as the water receded the ship was stranded high and dry with no way for the crew and passengers to get out. Devereaux, it seems, filled his purse with gold coins. Taking his logbook he jumped overboard before the ship was pushed into the cave, but he was found drowned on the beach after the storm passed by a beachcomber named Abe Trevanion. This was one of Tom Trevanion's distant great, great grandfathers and it was he had the headstone erected on the unmarked grave in the churchyard. He also purchased the point and the cove, never telling his relatives he owned it, and never sold it. It was the detective work of the local paper and the twins that found out that it had passed down through time to Tom."

"Is there any chance that we could take a look inside

the cave and see the ship for the viewers?"

"I can arrange that, but you will have to keep out of the way of the crew working down there."

"Is there any of the said treasure that we could video?"

"As luck would have it we have just uncovered a considerable amount of coins, both gold and silver that you may film from a distance."

"When you say considerable amount of coins, Cassie, how many are we talking about?"

"Oh, hundreds if not thousands, it looks like they were in a chest that has rotted away." The television crews were in turn taken down into the cave. Each one was taken aback by the size of the cave and the ship with its treasures. One of the camera crew asked Cassie how much is this treasure worth. "Many millions of pounds, but what we are learning about seventeenth century life aboard ship is immeasurable," said Cassie.

When everyone had finished work for the day, Manth and Benny locked the steel door over the cave entrance and returned to the cottage. Both Aunt Dora and Uncle Tom were already at home. Benny put the keys to the padlocks in the tin in the cupboard drawer. Tom said, "How did it go today with the press and the television people?"

"Cassie took care of most of it. They said it would be on the telly tonight and in the national papers tomorrow," said Manth.

That evening after the evening news the telephone

rang. "Hello, oh it's you," said Dora. She took the phone into the kitchen and carried on talking. When she returned to the front room she said to the twins, "Your mum and dad will be here on Friday to stay for a few days, then they are taking you home again."

"Taking us home again, why?"

"You two have been so wrapped up with what you've been doing, that you have lost all track of time. I'm afraid you only have this week left. The days and weeks have flown by and I'm afraid it's nearly time for you to be back at school."

"Tom could we come out on the boat tomorrow? It seems an age since we were out on the sea catching fish."

"If that is what you want to do, by all means. I'll give you a call in the morning."

"But what about the cave and the ship?"

"I'm pretty sure Pete and Cassie can manage perfectly well without your presence," said Tom. The next morning Tom gave the twins a call and they all had breakfast together for the first time in a while. They walked down to the harbour in the morning sunshine and climbed aboard Tom's boat. Ivan was already on board and, having everything ready they set off on the morning tide. Within a few minutes Benny and Manth were catching fish to bait the pots like they had never been away.

After the day on the boat, reliving the first few days of their holiday, the twins had dinner thinking about how few days they had left in this wonderful little Cornish village. The next morning the twins awoke to a beautiful day, just right for a day snorkelling at Frenchy's cove. Snorkelling had more or less been put on the back burner since they had first found the coin and pendant. Neither one of them would have changed a single moment of their summer holiday, but they both just wished it would last a little longer. Benny and Manth, after having their breakfast, put on their wetsuits, loaded all of their other things into their backpacks and headed for the cove. As they passed Rockfall point it was a hive of activity. The twins waved to the crew who were working bringing things up from the ship and loading them into vehicles for transport to the museum.

The sun was hot and the water cool and clear and sparkled as the sunlight reflected off of the small ripples on its surface. You could not imagine a better day for just swimming and lounging on the sandy beach. All too soon it was time to pack up their belongings and head back to the cottage. As they reached it, they met Tom, Eddie, Ivan and Alex all leaning against Eddie's jeep talking after a few hours in the cave. "How did it go today?" asked Manth. "We are making progress. We lifted out two of the port-side cannons and more coins this afternoon," said Eddie. "I am going to miss all of this," said Manth. "Why, are you going somewhere, Manth?" asked Alex. "I'm afraid it's time to go back home. Mum and dad are coming down on Friday and they are staying for a few days, then we are heading back to Norfolk."

"We shall miss seeing you about and catching the bait for the pots," said Ivan.

Friday arrived much too quickly for the twins, though they were of course excited about seeing their parents again after spending a great chunk of the summer down here in the west of the country. A few minutes after three in the afternoon their old Honda car pulled up in front of the cottage. Benny and Manth rushed out of the house to greet their mum and dad. "You look worn out," said Benny. "It's a long drive," said his dad, giving both of the twins a huge hug. "Mum, you look like you need a cup of tea," said Manth, putting her arm around her mother's waist and leading her towards the kitchen. Benny and his dad took the suitcases out of the car and carried them inside and up to the guest room, while Manth made a pot of tea.

"Where are Tom and Dora?" asked Tony. "Uncle Tom will be at Rockfall point and Aunt Dora will be home just after five," said Manth. "We saw you on the television. You both looked so grown up, with all of those reporters and television people. Did I hear one of them call you Manth?"

"Yes, mum for the last few weeks that has been my name."

"But you always insisted on being called Samantha!! Why the change of heart?"

"Kind of a long story, mum, but I quite like Manth. It's different." Dora arrived home greeting her sister with warm hugs, as they hadn't seen each other for what seemed like years. In fact it had been years, so there was a lot of catching up to do. "I'll get dinner started, then we can have a natter," said Dora. "I'll give you a hand. I've been sat in a car for hours on end and need something to do," said Joan. "Manth, take Tony down to Rockfall point and show him where the cave is. Tom should be on his way dreckly.

The twins took their dad down the road to Rockfall point, where everyone was just leaving the cave. Tom called them over to the entrance. "Tony, how are you? it's been an age. Care to take a look down the hole? We have a few minutes before Dora will have dinner ready." Tom, Tony and the twins descended into the cave and walked down to where the wreck was. It looked quite different from the last time the twins had been down here. "Things have moved on a bit in the last couple of days. Peter and Cassie are working wonders and with our help most of the valuable stuff has been removed. We are now sifting through what's left for the everyday things that the crew used."

"How much is all of this find worth, Tom?" asked Tony. "We are told on the open market it's worth millions. As far as I am aware there are no legal owners. All of it has been stolen from its owners by one group, only for it to be stolen from them. Then it was captured by Jacques, only for it to be buried underneath this piece of rock for over three hundred years. So as far as I know it now belongs to the twins and the land owner, that being me. We have had helpers who will have a small share each, but we all should come out a bit richer than when we started."

The village of course will become famous, which will

attract tourists and that is not a bad thing. Perhaps I can put a replica ship down here, scatter some fake coins about, have a video with screens telling the whole story from start to finish."

"That sounds like it might be a pretty good idea. You could have a tearoom/cafe down here, there is plenty of room and have a bit about the twins and how they found this place. I might even move down here and give you a hand," said Tony. Tom locked the steel doors and they walked back to the cottage. After dinner Tom asked Tony and Joan what their plans were for the few days they would be down here. Joan said she just wanted to chill out and catch some rays, as the kids would say. "What about you Tony?"

"I wouldn't mind a day or two out on the boat with you, Tom, if it's at all possible."

"Not a problem, Tony," answered Tom.

The next day Tony spent the day on the boat with Tom and Ivan, while Joan sunbathed on the sand at Frenchy's cove and the twins spent the day at Rockfall point. On Sunday Tom borrowed Eddie's jeep, as it was the only car that could carry them all and took them on a sightseeing tour. Monday was a repeat of Friday. Tuesday the twins said their good-byes to everyone, ready for their journey back to Norfolk the following day. Wednesday morning the mood was sombre around the breakfast table. The summer holiday was over, the adventure the twins had started they would play no further part in, although the work would carry on. They loaded all of the luggage into the car, and with hugs and tears they climbed aboard the Honda for the long trip to Norfolk. Just before they left Tom gave Benny a cardboard box. Inside were the blueprints for a model galleon and some parts that would help him start his own model. Tony started the car and they left Yarran's Shop for the last time this summer. Manth and Benny started their new term at their respective schools, enjoying their new-found fame after being on the television and having their pictures in the national papers. Soon the holiday faded into the past with schoolwork, homework and the day-to-day things that take over everyone's life.

It was one day in November that Tom phoned and told Joan, who had answered the phone, that the gold coin and the pendant that the twins had found, he had put into an auction after Cassie had given the all-clear to either keep them or sell them. The gold coin was extremely rare and sold for a five figure sum, the gold pendant sold to an anonymous person in Spain for half a million, mainly due to the name and date on the reverse and who the jeweller was. "I'll tell the twins when they come home from school," said Joan. "Also," said Tom, "ask Tony to give me a call anytime he has a spare moment."

"Nothing wrong, is there Tom?"

"No, no just something we talked about briefly when you were down here in the summer."

"Okay, Tom, I'll give him the message when he gets home later. Bye, love to Dora." When Manth and Benny came home from school, Joan told them about the auction and how much the items raised. Later when Tony arrived home from work, Joan told him that Tom would like a word when he had a moment.

Chapter X

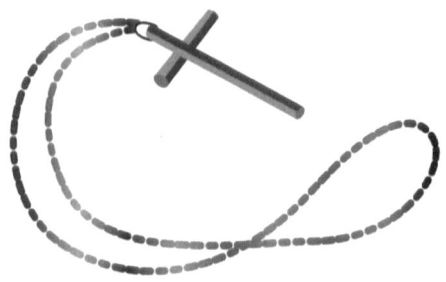

From that moment on, things began to change in the Franks home. Tom and Tony spent more and more time talking on the phone. Then one day a few days before Christmas, as they were sitting down to dinner Tony said, "How would you all like to go and live in Cornwall?" With surprised looks on everyone's faces they all agreed that it was an excellent idea. "But what about our, jobs, where would we live, where would Manth and Benny go to school, what will we live on?" asked Joan.

"Don't worry, that has all been taken care of. All I need to do is give Tom a call and tell him when we are coming down." It was agreed that they would tell Tom that they would put the house on the market straight away, both Tony and Joan would hand in their notices to their employers. Everything should be done by the end of January, so Tony phoned Tom and told him they would be in Cornwall by the first of February.

On the first of February, a cold and wet morning, Tony finished loading the Honda and they set off, stopping at the estate agent's office to give them the keys to the house. Then heading west they started the first day of the rest of their lives letting the cards fall as they may. After many hours of driving shared between Tony and Joan they arrived in the dark at the cottage in Yarran's Shop, Cornwall. Tom opened the front door and welcomed them while helping them with the luggage and Dora had a hot meal ready on the table. There were hugs all round, then they all sat down at the table and started eating. After the meal and the crockery was washed and put away the twins said good-night and went to bed.

Tom, Dora, Tony and Joan sat in the lounge with coffee, relaxing after an exhausting day driving. Tom outlined the plans for the telling of the story of the Chasing the Sea Hound exhibition. "We have the backing of the council and I have even secured a grant, plus we have planning permission to have an exhibition hall and restaurant in the cave. I will go into this more deeply tomorrow after you've had a good night's rest. There is no rush to get up in the morning, just treat the cottage like home." The next morning after breakfast Joan took the twins to the local secondary school to enrol them, asking if they could start at the beginning of the next week. It was agreed that they would start at the school on Monday.

Next they went to see Dora, as Joan had never seen Dora's shop. Dora asked her if she would like to work part time in the shop until things got under way with the work at the cave. Joan said that she would do some hours, but she would do it for free in return for staying with her and Tom. Joan then wanted to have a look inside the cave, as she had never been down there, so they parked the car at the cottage and walked to Rockfall point. Manth and Benny took her down into the cave and introduced her to Cassie. Joan was amazed at the size of the cave. She had never realized just how big it was. Cassie showed her some of the things that they were now finding, everyday items that the crew of a seventeenth-century sailing ship used. They had found the compass and the sextant, the remains of guns, swords and oil lamps, combs, plates, knives, boots and shoes. Cassie treated these things as though the were worth a king's ransom.

Cassie was excited about what Tom had told her about his plans for the exhibition. She was hoping Tom would let her and the museum play a part in it's creation. Manth said that she would put in a good word for her. It was now lunchtime so they returned to the cottage. In the afternoon Tom, Eddie, Ivan and Alex called in to the cottage on their way to Rockfall point, "Is anyone coming to the cave?" asked Tom. Benny said, "Yes," and Manth said, "I'll stay with mum if that's alright."

"Your choice," replied Tom. The five of them walked to the cave and descended into its depth, where Cassie was sweeping the area with a metal detector. "I'm glad you are here," she said. "We have finished removing all of the seventeenth-century items, so Tom, the cave is now yours."

"What about all of the ship's timbers?" asked Tom. "We have photographs of the wreck. Do with them as you wish. I would hope that some of the better timbers could be used in your proposed exhibition, Tom," answered Cassie. "We were hoping you might like to be involved in our plans," said Tom. "Please, Cassie," said Benny. "I would be very pleased to," said Cassie with a beaming face.

The next morning Tom phoned his friend, Tel, "Tel, how are you fixed to do some work for me?"

"What have you in mind, Tom?" asked Tel, who was at a bit of a loose end, it being the middle of winter and not a lot of work about. "Well, to start with, in the Rockfall point cave there are tons of timber that needs sorting. As you have probably seen on the television and the papers, it was a French corsair's ship. We need to sort the good timber from the rotten, burning what is useless. Would you be interested?"

"I'll be there dreckly," said Tel.

Tel arrived half an hour later and Tom, Manth and Benny walked with him to Rockfall point. Tom unlocked the steel door of the cave. "I wondered what was here when Boom Boom blasted a hole in this rock for you," said Tel. Tom replied apologetically, "I'm sorry I couldn't tell you at the time, it was all a bit hush, hush."

They all descended into the cave. Tom had installed a new lighting system, as the village Christmas street lights had had to be returned for the festive season. They walked down to where the old ship had been resting since 1683. "Right, Tel, keep all of the oak beams that are still usable and all of the timber that is rotten take outside and have a bonfire. I have big plans for this cave and you, Tel, could have work here for the next year or two if you want it. I have some architect drawings that have been approved by the planning department in the cottage if you care to have a look." Tel phoned his work crew and told them to meet him at Tom's cottage right away. They all walked back to the cottage, Tom and Tel looked at the drawings spread out on the kitchen table. "It's a big job, Tom, I will need to get some expert help and that costs, Tom."

"We have a grant and some money," said Tom. "Who are this, we, Tom?" inquired Tel.

"Well, two of them are stood here, Manth and Benny, Tony and Joan, their parents, are the others."

Work started when Tel's crew arrived. All through the next eighteen months Rockfall point was turned into a hive of activity with lorries carrying bricks, tiles, glass and everything that goes into building an underground exhibition hall complete with restaurant and reception area. A half-sized replica of the Chien de Mer was built and installed. The twins marvelled at the changes to the cave every time they went down there. Cassie and Peter helped with displays of the lives of seventeenth-century sailors, complete with pictures of how they dressed and some of the relics from the actual ship. Two of the original ship's cannons stood in the reception area on refurbished mounts. Large photographs of Manth and Benny, along with their story of the discovery, adorned the walls. There was also a wall dedicated to the story of the Dinero Espriito and captain Carlos Sanchez where the whole story began. In a glass display case were the items that Tom had buried under the slab in his garden.

On a warm summer's day in June the subterranean exhibition of the treasure ship the Sea Hound opened its doors to the public and the world's media. The little Cornish village of Yarran's Shop was once again, with Manth and Benny Franks, the talking point of the nation. Eddie, dressed in a suit, along with Ivan and Alex, now wearing a wedding ring, joined Cassie, Peter, Tom and Dora showing the local dignitaries around the different exhibits. That evening there was a party in the new restaurant for all of those who had helped in the creation of this exhibition centre. As the night turned into morning Manth and Benny went to their beds tired but elated, the result of their dream come true.

The End

Acknowledgements

Jim Burns, my email friend and editor in Jacksonville, Florida, without whose help this story may never have made it to the pages of this book.

Brett Thorn, at the Bucks museum Aylesbury for answering some treasure questions.

Tasha Fullbrook, the finds liaison officer at Helston, Cornwall for taking time out in her new job to be of assistance to me.

Any mistakes are mine alone.
I apologize wholeheartedly.

- James Gordon -

*Available worldwide from Amazon
and all good bookstores*

Michael Terence
Publishing

www.mtp.agency

www.facebook.com/mtp.agency

@mtp_agency

www.ingramcontent.com/pod-product-compliance
Lightning Source LLC
LaVergne TN
LVHW091544060526
838200LV00036B/694